Tales from the
Emerald Mountains:
Dig Within

Tales from the Emerald Mountains: Dig Within

Rhett DeVane

Tales from the Emerald Mountains:
Dig Within
© 2014 Rhett DeVane
All rights reserved

Date of first publication: October 7, 2014
Published by Writers4Higher
Tallahassee, Florida

Cover design by Elizabeth Babski, Babski Creative Studios

ISBN-13: 978-0692302293

ISBN-10: 0692302298

Printed in the United States of America

Dedication

To my readers, near and far. May the Light always go with you.

Acknowledgements

Rhett wishes to thank the following people:

The Wild Women Writers group for their expertise and friendship.

Gina Edwards: amazing editor and friend.

Elizabeth Babski: talented artist, cover designer, and friend.

All of my loving friends who continue to boost and support me.

Her readers. Without you, her words go to waste.

Her family, both the blood ties and otherwise ties.

And to the universe, for sending muses to light her way.

The Clan Family Tree

Elsbeth The First Mother

- Jen » Faith
- Mari
- Taka-Herb
- Jondu

Sim The First Father

- Grant » Zeke
- Slate
- Gabby
- Brick

Chapter One

Elsbeth The First Mother watched the mountain man.

Same scrawny dwarf with hair like a dump rat's pelt and an unkempt beard to match. Since she and her friend Sim had escaped from New Haven City, Elsbeth had seen Taproot through fifty Emerald Mountain springs. He acted stranger than usual this year.

"What's up with you, *old* man?"

The favorite joke between them failed to gain his usual snipped laugh. Funny since she was over a half-century old too, not exactly a kid. Instead, Taproot crammed cloth bags of dried herbs into his backpack. He took a swig of tonic made especially for shaking off the winter doldrums and turned his attention toward Elsbeth. "Got something to do."

What kind of *something*? Elsbeth scanned Taproot's cavern. Larger than hers or any of the other burrows of her clan. Earthen walls with stocked shelves, a kitchen area with a hearth and storage bins, sitting stones rounded by years in the nearby stream, and a flat rock table. On the other side, a living area spread out, with a sofa made from layers of stacked rocks and down-stuffed cushions. Unlike her burrow, Taproot's had a second room, a combination library and sleeping area.

Of course, Taproot needed more space. He was over three feet tall. Elsbeth had to stretch to reach four inches. He didn't treat her or any of the clan as if their diminished size mattered, though. Easy to overlook their differences when magic ran through them all.

Elsbeth studied the root-laced earthen ceiling with its series of skylights fashioned from green and amber dump-dive glass bottles buried bottoms-up. Their filtered light met the ever-present shine from the foxfire clumps below. The light-absorbing fungus illuminated the cave with a soft green glow.

Taproot's cavern, beneath the hollow stump hiding the topside entrance, held its own special aroma: a blend of herbs and the musty earth. Elsbeth took a deep breath. That smell whispered *home* to her spirit, much more than any place had back in New Haven City, years ago when she had been a scared little girl named Elizabeth.

Taproot's burrow needed a few dried flowers, some artwork. All of her spirit-daughters' homes brimmed with color, except for Jondu's. That spirit-child never stayed inside her cave long enough to wish for decoration.

Elsbeth had tried to help the magician out in the cave-improvement department over the years, to no good end. Like Sim The First Father and his unruly brood of boys, Taproot preferred his hovel "without princess-y touches."

"I know we'll have to harvest when the new plants come in." Elsbeth finally addressed his *something-to-do* statement. She waved a hand toward four long beams draped with hanging dried herbs. "But we have plenty still left from last season. So what's with the dither?"

"Dither?" The mountain magician chortled. Bits of dried rosemary and snips of other herbs showered from his beard. No telling what else lived in there. "You never fail to amuse me with your funny lowlander sayings, Princess."

Elsbeth barely recalled the ten-year-old scared orphan she had once been. For one thing, she was so small now, a sort of creature Taproot called a *one-spirit*. Able to live off what the mountains provided. Hide in the protective caverns carved beneath the surface. And dive in a landfill for supplies without so much as a sniffle over the stench. Plus, she had a family now. A big one.

Elsbeth helped herself to tonic in a doll-sized cup she had rescued from a dump-dive the first summer she and Sim came to the valley. A deep chip marred one edge. She drank from the opposite side, flinched, and added a drop of wildwood honey. Most of Taproot's tonics bit her tongue, once she got past their unusual smell. This one held hints of dirt, wild plum, rosehips, and something a little fishy.

"I don't even much remember *being* a lowlander," Elsbeth said.

"Guess fifty years is long enough to forget being one of their sort," Taproot said. "I have to remind myself I once lived amongst them." He turned his attention to his pack. "And fifty years is long enough for a little one such as you to figure things out." He waggled four fingers in the air, as if he scattered glitter with his hand. "*Live* on the outside. *Learn* on the inside."

Elsbeth let out a snort. Why did the old dwarf have to speak in riddles? Perhaps by the time she reached Taproot's age—two, three hundred, or more?—Elsbeth would riddle too.

Before Elsbeth could fire off questions, Jen dashed into the room, all flowing robes and golden hair. Her spirit-daughter. Elsbeth hated to admit she had a favorite, but Jen had been her first-born—if *born* was the right word for a pointy-eared little girl who emerged from a cocoon, turned magic crystal.

"Sim says the trails are clear enough!" Jen jiggled from one foot to the other. Her birth crystal medallion bobbed against her robe like a fallen leaf caught in a whirlpool. Poor little creature growing inside had to be dizzy. Where did Jen find such boundless energy? She barely stopped long enough to eat or sleep.

All four of Elsbeth's spirit-daughters were different, like the freckles across her own nose. Part of her, but no two exactly alike.

"Take a breath. Calm down. Let's talk this over." Taproot motioned Jen toward the kettle. "Help yourself to some tonic, wild girl."

Jen flicked a quick frown, an unusual expression for her. Then she grinned and dashed to the hearth to pour a cup. Some spilled over the rim and sucked into the earthen floor. Taproot and Elsbeth exchanged exasperated glances.

"We can go today! Just think! It's been five months." Jen did the little dance-step again. More tonic sloshed out. "Probably all kinds of treasures there by now." Her eyes twinkled. "Chocolate and cookies and books and art supplies and . . ." The rest of her words got lost in twirls and hops.

True, lowlanders cast off all kinds of things. Amidst the rotting banana peels, maggots, and papers, the landfill held surprises ready to discover.

"What do you think, Taproot?" Elsbeth asked. Jen ceased her jiving and stared at the two of them, her eyes wide.

The mountain man stopped packing and settled onto a sitting stone. "What do *you* think, Elsbeth?"

He usually called her *Princess* and seldom asked her opinion. More strange behaviors. Taproot made all the important decisions. Especially since the soldiers now occupied the next valley. The old city dump was no more. Paved over, with long rows of metal barracks on top like a bubbly, gray rash. The lowlanders had carved another landfill three miles distant. A much longer trek for the clan, and they had to camp overnight near the river to make the scavenging trips worthwhile.

Elsbeth shrugged. *She* certainly wasn't in charge, nor did she wish to be.

Taproot pointed a bony finger at her. "You *know* the answer. Quit acting slow-witted. Dig within."

The *slow-witted* comment stung. After a long winter, the old magician could be crotchety, like her. A narrow tunnel connected the clan quarters to Taproot's cavern, but they were all under a long-standing order to leave him alone during the winter months. Sim The First Father called him *Tap-rude*. Elsbeth would never say that to the old man's face, though it often applied.

She sat down on a stone and stuffed down her hurt feelings. "The landfill is pretty far. There's a river and a high pass between here and there. That route probably still has snow and ice." She tapped her chin. "We wouldn't have much cover from the hawks, yet."

Taproot's eyebrows danced like two irritated wooly worms. "And . . ."

"And . . . we probably need to wait a few weeks. Maybe . . ." Elsbeth searched Taproot's features for approval then continued when he did not react. "Maybe when the ice melts in the upper reaches of the stream and the brush takes on new leaves."

Jen stomped. "Sim The First Father and the boys aren't going to like this."

Taproot leaned back, took a long draw from his cup. "Safe *is* better than dead."

Elsbeth let out her trapped breath. Had she gotten the answer right?

"Sim is often brash." Taproot nodded toward Elsbeth. "You'll have to ride herd over his daring-do."

Daring-do. Taproot's odd word summed up Sim. He would dash headlong with one of his flint-tipped spears, ready to take on danger. Snakes, bears, hawks. Sim figured he could conquer them all with his swagger. Amazing, he was still on this side of the Light.

Elsbeth stood and smoothed her robe, pocked with holes from the long winter's wear. She'd have to drop by Mari's burrow for a fitting. No need to sew anymore, since her second spirit-daughter loved to design and could fashion clothing from any scrap of dump-dive material. "Like *I* can control Sim."

Maybe things would be different if she and Sim were a bit more like lowlanders, with two spirits joining to create children and then sharing decisions for the clan. But they weren't. Her daughters arose from her spirit. Sim's sons came from his.

Of course that had advantages. Sim didn't control her either, though often he tried.

"You'll find a way to rein Sim in, Princess." Taproot slapped his hands on his skinny thighs. "You'll have to. I'm leaving."

Elsbeth felt the tonic's warmth drain from her body. "Wh . . . What?"

"High time I go for a walkabout." Taproot tipped his head toward his packs. "Thought I'd depart after the Spring Festival."

"But, but . . . where are you going?" Elsbeth's mouth felt as if dandelion fluff coated her tongue.

"Been over seventy-five springs since I went on a trek. Planned on going before. Then you and Sim showed up. You two changed my plans, for a bit." He frowned at his hands, then retrieved an oak twig from his pocket and used it to plow dirt from beneath his fingernails. "Figure I'll try to find my old friend Dell-Fee."

Dell-Fee. Elsbeth knew the name. She was one of the circus performers who had escaped with Taproot into the valley, years before Elizabeth and Simon fled New Haven City for the Emerald Mountains. Before they became Elsbeth and Sim.

Elsbeth recalled the fantastical saga of Dell-Fee, one of Taproot's harrowing dwarf troupe escapades, but figured it to be another of the mountain magician's tall tales. So much of what he said seemed a stretch of truth.

"Might check on the deep mountain clans while I'm at it," Taproot added.

Others like them. One-spirits. Somewhere, far away. If Elsbeth longed for travel, like her spirit-daughter Jondu, she might beg to tag along, but the thought of moving from this protected valley chilled her blood.

"You can't leave us here by ourselves!" Jen said before Elsbeth could get the same words out.

Taproot leaned down so that his burly head was inches from their faces. "You aren't alone, second little princess. You have a clan ten strong, the protection of the Pensworthy owls, and the friendship of the animals." He paused. "Except for the hawks and bears. I'd still watch out for them, if I was you."

Elsbeth's heart thumped so hard, she could hear blood swoosh in her ears. "But we can't survive without you, Taproot."

The mountain magician tapped Elsbeth's forehead with one fingertip. "Everything you need, you have in there, in your little princess noggin." He stretched to his full height and rubbed the small of his back. "I'm hitting the trail."

Jondu waited until she heard no noise from the clan. She slipped into the tunnel to the girls' *necessary room*, a place where they deposited their bodily wastes. What better spot to hide a secret exit tunnel? Most of the one-spirits came and went so fast, they wouldn't take time to look behind the tattered flap of dark material, hidden in a recess off the first turn.

She wondered who had carved the small hole. Had to be Sim The First Father, the only one-spirit bold enough. A couple of winters back, Jondu had observed him coming and going from both the male and female necessary room tunnels. Spreading Taproot's powdered herbs to contain the smell, he explained once when she asked. Jondu didn't buy that bag of hooey. Bet there was a matching exit tunnel on the boys' side too.

No matter. If it *was* Sim, she privately sang his praises. The main tunnel exits caked with ice soon after the Fall Festival. Taproot's hollow gathered drifts of snow too, cutting off all routes topside.

Jondu could only pace the underground caves for so long. Her body twitched with the need to breathe topside air.

She stopped long enough to listen for any sounds before slipping beneath the burlap. Now she knew how moles felt. No foxfire or hearth's glow lit this deep passageway. Jondu felt her way along, curving first left, then right. Finally, a sliver of light pierced the darkness and she moved faster, toward topside. A boulder protected the tunnel opening from the cutting wind and snowdrifts. Perfect. She wiggled from the exit and stood.

"Who-wee!" The sound came out before she could remind herself to remain quiet. Jondu clamped her hands over her mouth. No telling if hungry predators lurked. The trees snapped and clicked under the weight of icicles. In the snow-muted silence, a hawk screeched. The fine danger hairs prickled on Jondu's neck. Had to pay attention to that fuzz. It had saved her on many occasions, long before her other senses sounded the alarm.

So much for going for a long hike. The hawk was too close. Jondu would make a nice, late-winter snack. She sat cross-legged on the frozen ground, happy to be topside for a few stolen moments, even if the cold chilled her to shivers.

Wonder where the other tunnel comes out? Has to be close. She stood and stepped into the open long enough to survey the area. Jondu noted a series of tiny divots where feet had tapped down the surface. Ah-ha! Sim had been up here too. She looked closer. Two sets of prints. Bet they belonged to Sim and Jen. Who else besides her had the courage to come topside before the thaw?

Just our little secret, fellow adventurers. I won't tell.

The other one-spirits had their distinct roles. Sim The First Father and Jen lived to dump-dive for supplies and treasures. Grant liked to read and ponder deep thoughts. Brick spent his time writing the history of the clan and forming fantastic tales. Gabby strummed one of his many instruments and sang ballads. Slate interpreted dreams and visions. Mari designed clothing. Taka-Herb took the part of healer. And Elsbeth? Well, Elsbeth was the all-knowing First Mother, of course.

Everyone fit into the clan. Except for her.

"One day, I'll go," she whispered to no one. "Far, far from this valley. Take the trails leading deep into the Emerald Mountains."

Jondu felt the truth resound inside, as deep and steady as her heartbeat. She was born to be one of the travelers.

Chapter Two

Sim The First Father used a flint knife blade to scrape the ice from the bottom of his shoes. Other than providing time to knap new spear tips or practice his whittling, winter was a huge bore. And it lasted too long in the Emerald Mountains. All that time trapped in the underground caves wore on his nerves, no matter that the living quarters were much roomier than the first cramped burrow he and Elsbeth had shared during the early years.

Grant, Sim's first spirit-son, stood with his thumbs hooked under his pack straps. His dark skin, hair, and eyes provided a stark contrast to the snow. "I think we shouldn't travel over Mad Man's Pass."

Of course. Grant The Thinker always mulled things through. Worried. Planned. Perhaps Jen might've been a better fit for the first hike of the season. She was as carefree and adventurous as Sim. What was Elsbeth's word for the two of them? Ah, yes. *Reckless.*

When Sim squinted toward the clear skies overhead, wind fingered through the evergreens, rattled the barren limbs of an aged hickory tree, then dipped down to push back the sprigs of blond hair hanging across his brows. His blue eyes watered. Back in their home valley, a few splashes of new growth peeked through the leaf-strewn ground, but here, many feet higher, the cold dead season still held life captive. He snugged his scarf closer to his neck.

"Let's check it out from Taproot's watchtower." Sim slipped the sheathed knife back into a jacket pocket and turned around, taking an easterly direction. Sim motioned for Grant to follow, stepping into the depressions made by his feet. "The second one in line always has the easier path."

"Unless that person follows *your* path, which may or may *not* be easy," Grant said.

They slogged up a series of switchbacks, then back down. At an embankment dotted with massive stones, Sim ascended. Near the precipice, he veered, squeezing into a narrow split in the rock. In a few feet, the slit opened onto a high plateau: Taproot's watchtower. They dropped their packs and took deep breaths of the fresh chilled air.

"This place always amazes me," Sim said. "On a clear day, you can see the edge of the boulder field near the new landfill."

Grant shivered and swung his head to look in the opposite direction. "Sure provides a good view of the army base."

Anger clawed at Sim's gut, as it always did when he thought of soldiers. His father had been a military man during the last area war, back in New Haven City. "Far as I'm concerned, the ground can open up and swallow the whole place, army and all. Let it sink into the garbage dump it was built upon."

If his military father hadn't been the leader of the resistance, he might still be alive, and Sim would be full-grown by now. Sim did the math. As a human lowlander, he would be sixty-one! Wow.

Sim shook his head. Long time ago. He tried not to think about soldiers. Sure, he pilfered their cast-offs. Found some good stuff. But overall, soldiers were to be avoided.

"I remember that first landfill," Grant said. "It was good."

"If it wasn't for their stupid base, we wouldn't have to worry about Mad Man's Pass. We could make it to the dump and back in a few hours and still have plenty of dive time."

The two stood side by side, lost in private thoughts for a moment. Other than the whumps from melting snow clots bombing the ground, the mountains rested. Silent gods.

"There's still ice cover at Mad Man's Pass." Sim picked up a palm-sized rock and pitched it hard. It nicked bark from a nearby pine before rappelling to the ground and landing with a muffled thud.

Grant tipped his head in the direction of their home valley. "Elsbeth said—"

"I know what Lizard the Lousy said." He hated to admit Elsbeth was right, about *any*thing. "Doesn't make it law." After all, Sim was a year and two whole months older. Meant he was wiser too. Right?

"Still, I—"

"I say, we press on." Sim shouldered his pack. "Bound to be a rabbit run or game trail through that pass, by now. We're not the only ones moving around."

Mari rolled up her measuring tape, a treasured dump-dive find. She gathered her long dark hair and secured it with a snippet of faded blue lace. "Looks like you've gained in the middle section, First Mother."

Elsbeth pressed her lips into a thin line. Had to be the tall stacks of acorn flour pancakes slathered with wildwood honey. Winter brought on boredom, even with books and study and gabbing with her clan. Food provided comfort. "Good thing warmer weather is on the way. I must crawl from these caves and get some exercise, or end up as wide as I am tall."

When Mari laughed, Elsbeth heard the shadowy echo of her own mother's mirth. How did the one-spirit magic work? The two tears Elsbeth had gathered into the moth cocoon and worn close to her heart thirty winters ago—had they formed during a time when Elsbeth longed for her own mother? She held few clear memories of her parents, but somewhere inside, their essence must still exist. Hints of them lived on in Elsbeth's spirit-daughters, like Mari's musical laughter.

When this *younger* had emerged from her birth crystal that long-ago spring, Elsbeth immediately knew her name. Mari. Same as the loving mother she once had, before the last area war and those awful soldiers.

Elsbeth thought of her other offspring. How had all of them turned out so physically different from her? She touched one of her long dark braids. None of Elsbeth's spirit-daughters had the creamy caramel skin similar to her own mother's, yet pale enough for the swish of nose freckles to show. And shamrock green eyes from her Irish father. He used to tell Elsbeth she was "the perfect sweet blend of light and dark."

Taka-Herb was the third spirit-daughter. Originally named Herb because of the child's love of all things green, then nicknamed Taka-Herb after her habit of filching dried herbs and stuffing them into her pockets. As she grew older, Taka-Herb developed a knack for healing. Again, a trait definitely from Elsbeth's mother. Simply the sight of blood made Elsbeth's stomach go wiggly.

But Jondu? For sure, her fourth spirit-daughter's edgy wanderlust mirrored Elsbeth's father. Ready to go on any quest. So many times in Jondu's first years, Elsbeth and Sim had led a frantic search for the lost younger. Small wonder Jondu hadn't fallen prey to a night stalker. Good thing the Pensworthy owls watched over them.

"I have some lovely linen, printed with little yellow and red posies, though the colors are a bit faded." Mari rummaged in a wooden chest and lifted a thick square of folded material. "Think it might have been some kind of lowlander's table covering. Has a few stains I couldn't remove, but plenty of good. Even with your extra, um, girth, I'll get robes for all four of us from this, plus one for Jen's new, little spirit-daughter." Mari hugged the material to her. "Isn't it exciting? We've waited ten springs for two new youngers!"

"A long time. Yes. But we can't create so many that nature suffers under our numbers." Taproot had advised this after the births of Grant and Jen. Too many beings had long been the curse of the lowlanders. Their cities crawled with the underfed and homeless.

Elsbeth didn't truly understand how the one-spirit magic worked. How two tears collected inside a moth cocoon at a time of great emotion and kept close to the heart for six long winter months could turn into another distinct being. She had no idea how Sim created his spirit-sons, with one of his many rocks rather than in a crystalized cocoon.

Shrinking in size, Taproot explained, doubled the creative impulse inside the birth parent. Beings like her and Sim no longer needed another to spawn new life. Sim and

Elsbeth had four spirit-children apiece. Now the time had arrived for their children to create life too.

Elsbeth clasped her hands together. This year, this special spring, Jen and Grant would add their offspring to the clan. Bless the Light!

If Elsbeth had her true wish, each spring would bring several new one-spirits, until the clan grew and grew and grew. She imagined a network of caves spreading across the valley, filled with her and Sim's kin. But because their concentrated life flames promised long lives, she and Sim had cemented a law into place. Only two new births per ten years. One male. One female.

Everything was about balance.

This spring, Jen's first spirit-daughter would emerge into the Emerald Mountains. Would she share Jen's wild spirit? Could the clan stand two such reckless creatures? Three, if she counted Sim.

"Just think, Mari. In ten years, at the next birth-spring, it will be *your* turn." Elsbeth smiled. Any spirit-daughter of Mari's would be a welcome addition. Kindness glowed around Mari like a halo.

"I know I—"

"Elsbeth! Elsbeth!" A voice called out. They turned toward the cave's entrance tunnel.

Sim's second spirit-son, Slate, skidded to a halt. He gulped air.

"What . . . ?" Elsbeth stepped over to him.

"My dream!" he managed between ragged breaths. "My dream!" Slate paced back and forth. His shoulders quivered.

Mari guided him to a sitting stone. "Calm yourself, Slate. I'll pour you a cup of chamomile tea."

Elsbeth took a seat across from him. This one-spirit possessed The Sight. How he had landed such a gift from Sim's restless spirit defied logic. Hard to tell if this reaction was excitement or fear. Slate emoted equally with both.

The clan owed much to Slate's visions. They had found new wild bee hollows, dewberry patches thick with fruit, and upon occasion, the location of some amazing dump-dive find.

Mari handed over two cups of steaming tea, then decanted one for herself. The scent of chamomile calmed Elsbeth even before she took the first sip. They sat around Mari's tablerock for a few minutes before anyone spoke, the best approach to take when dealing with Slate.

"Now," Mari said, "Tell us about this dream."

He set the teacup down so hard, the pale brown liquid lapped over the edges. "I saw blood and death!" His hands shook. "I saw tears and crying!"

Mari's brows crimped together. "Has to be a vision of those awful lowlander wars again. Will they never learn?"

His pale face mirrored horror. "No. No! It was us!"

Chapter Three

Sim stood at the jagged edge of Mad Woman Gorge. "More water in the river than I anticipated."

The gorge harbored a legend, as did most places in the Emerald Mountains. If Taproot's story was true, some poor soul had jumped to her death at this very spot. Each time Sim paused here, he imagined her swirling and tumbling like a fallen leaf until her body dashed against the boulders at the base of Mad Woman Falls. Sim thought of the waterway as female, too. An angry one. Even when he riled Elsbeth by calling her Lizard the Lousy, she was mild in comparison to these waters.

It had been a record year for snowfall. Seven feet according to the measuring tree next to Taproot's hollow. Mad Woman River posed a challenge even in a meager snowmelt year. Now, with the spring thaw, she coursed through the rock gorge as wicked and unruly as her name.

"The bridge has been compromised." Grant motioned toward the narrow outcropping of stones where the clan usually found passage. "I think we should turn back."

"That's your problem, Grant. You think *waaaay* too much." Sim dropped his pack and slogged to the edge of the gorge, leaning to study the curving riverbanks. "There! See? A birch sapling has fallen across, a few feet downstream. We can use it for our bridge."

Sim snatched up his pack and settled it into place. Grant snapped two extra clips to secure his own pack. When they reached the uprooted tree, Sim tested his weight on the trunk. "Must've come down in the last storm. It's still green and strong. I could waltz a full-grown mountain bear across and it'd hold."

Grant hung back until Sim reached the halfway point. The tree shifted. Its limbs slapped the water, sending spray clapping against the rocks. Sim flung out his arms, teetered for a breath-stopping moment, then whooped. He scampered the rest of the way and jumped onto the far bank. He turned and motioned. "Hey, whatcha waiting on?"

Inching along, Grant crossed in slow, even steps. A couple of times, his feet slipped on small chunks of ice still crusted on the sapling's bark.

"Gah!" Sim called. "Even Elsbeth could make it faster!"

Grant reached the halfway spot and paused. The river swirled over rounded boulders, creating a dull roar. For a second, he froze. Then Sim watched him step until he was close enough to leap to solid ground.

"Good job." Sim clamped Grant on the shoulder. "Sometimes you have to stop thinking so much and just *go*."

As they moved farther from the river and ascended, snowbanks towered on either side of the narrow game trail. The air grew more chilled. The musical ting of water dripping from branch tips joined the low rumble from the river behind them.

"Keep the prize in mind," Sim said. "Once we reach Mad Man's Pass, we'll be on the downslope. We can camp, and spend all day tomorrow dump-diving."

"Elsbeth won't be happy when she discovers we're gone." Grant shifted his pack. "And you know Taproot doesn't approve of travel until well after the Spring Festival."

Sim tore off a hunk of dried plum, offered a bite to Grant, then chewed. "Lizard will get over it. She always does. I'll find something in that dump to appease her. Maybe some books or chocolate bars. And as for our old mountain man, he's too caught up in rules. Always has been."

When his spirit-son didn't reply, Sim motioned to the pendant suspended from a piece of woven jute around Grant's neck. "Don't worry. I'll have you back in plenty of time for the birth of your spirit-son."

Elsbeth forced herself to remain calm until she had brushed through the suspended strips of cloth marking Mari's doorway. No need to make Mari or Slate any more distressed. She entered the main tunnel and broke into a jog.

That dream can't be about us, she told herself. *Can't be!*

As she scurried by her other three spirit daughters' burrows, she mentally tallied their names: Jen, Taka-Herb, Jondu. Wilted purple mountain asters bordered Jen's doorway. Taka-Herb's held fragrant sprigs of dried rosemary tied with twine. Smoothed river rock hoodoos teetered in piles next to Jondu's door. Then her own threshold, decorated with her line drawings tacked in place next to the wooden nameplate.

So much to do in preparation for the Spring Festival. Add to that, worry over Taproot's announcement. He couldn't leave them! Now this.

If Slate's visions were true, only one person could cause such drama: Sim. Elsbeth had to find him, give him a stern warning against whatever harebrained thing he planned before it was too late. Like the time he snuck into a hibernating bear's den on a dare. Or the summer he body-surfed Mad Woman River and nearly ended up sluicing over the falls. Or the time . . . She halted the list. It could go on for a while. Fifty years of lunacy.

I simply don't have patience for tears and crying and . . . Elsbeth shivered . . . *blood.* And *death.* She stalled in her tracks, frozen by the word.

Magic could solve a number of things. Death, Taproot assured her, was not one of them. She willed her legs to move again.

Two unadorned holes led off to her left and right. The *necessary rooms*, Taproot's term for bathrooms. Though those cavern tunnels wound back and forth for several feet, enough to contain the rank smell, she automatically picked up her pace when she passed.

Elsbeth reached the threshold of the Common Hall, the shared room between the homes of the daughters and sons. Warmed by a massive double hearth, the spirit of the cozy cave calmed her a bit.

For many seasons, this room had held laughter, talk, and the aroma of good food: greens fresh from the banks of the stream, plums simmered in honey, toasty breads hot from the stone oven by the hearth. A pot of stew steamed on the rock stove—turnip roots and carrots if she trusted her chilled nose. Someone would make acorn flour bread to go along, too. Probably Sim's fourth spirit-son doing the cooking, she hoped. Brick cooked the best of the boys. Sim rushed everything and often burned the meals.

Gabby, Sim's third spirit-son, glanced up from his *doo-brood*—a carved, oblong wooden instrument strung with spun rabbit hair. He plucked a chord. "Elsbeth. What's—?"

"Where's Sim?" She crossed the room and stood with her arms propped on her hips.

"I've been here practicing for the festival for a while. Haven't seen him." Gabby strummed a few notes. "*She wanders in the mists of the willow's breath pond,*" he crooned. "*Her hair tipped with moon, her face shone upon.*"

Any other time, Elsbeth would be happy to flop down on a sitting rock and listen. Gabby's silken voice mesmerized her. His folksy ballads took her to faraway lands filled with damsels and dragons and heroes. Just not now.

Brick huddled over his notepad, close enough to the hearth to use the flickering light. Elsbeth bustled to his side of the room. "Have you seen him?"

Brick frowned. Took a breath and puffed it back out. Looked up. Everyone knew not to bother the scribe when he was creating. And Brick was always creating, when he wasn't reading any kind of printed material gleaned from a dump-dive. "Seen who, or is it whom?" His brows furrowed. "I often confuse the two."

A snake could slither down the tunnels into the Common Room, coil up beside the hearth, jangle his rattler, stretch his mouth wide open with fangs dripping with poison, and Brick wouldn't notice.

"Sim! That's whom, or who, or . . ." Elsbeth stomped one foot. "Whatever."

"You appear . . ." Brick tapped his chin with a stub of a pencil. His red hair stuck out in clownish tufts. ". . . Perplexed.

Mystified." He hummed, drilling the end of the pencil on his chin. "No, befuddled! You definitely look *beeeeeee*-fuddled. I love that word." He scratched the pencil tip across the page.

Hope he wasn't writing poetry. What could possibly rhyme with *befuddled*? Cuddled? Muddled? Troubled? No, troubled didn't quite fit.

Stop! She scolded herself.

You have the mind of a scrambled squirrel. On task, Elsbeth, on task! Taproot often told her when her attention split off in different directions. She had hoped, after all of these years, she would think like an adult. But the magic didn't work that way.

"Well then, what about Grant?" Elsbeth idled in place.

"Let's see . . ." More chin tapping. "Did I see him today? Or was it last night?"

Slate slid into the Common Hall and skidded to a halt. His thin face flushed pink. Elsbeth shot him a stern *shush!* look and moved her head side to side. His pale brows crimped together, but he didn't speak.

"I can't believe you have no clue where they are." Elsbeth huffed. "Not like this place is vast."

"Is it my purpose to keep up with everyone? I think not." Brick shuffled his papers until the edges lined up. "I have worlds to wander."

Elsbeth envied Brick a little. Some of his fantasy talent would come in handy during the long winter months when all she saw were the dirt walls of their burrows, the same faces day after day, and an occasional earthworm.

Elsbeth spun around and left the hall, heading toward the boys' quarters.

"That girl's gone winter-wild." One of them said it and the others agreed. Elsbeth didn't bother to whip back around and offer an argument. Yes, she was a little cave-bound, but who wasn't? When she was able to crawl to the surface, she planned to kiss the ground, even if it stood ankle deep in melting snow muck.

The first doorway on the right barely showed amidst the clutter of rocks, stacks of cut oak branches, and knurls of mountain ash. Elsbeth turned in and followed the narrow tunnel until it opened to a cave the same size as hers.

Elsbeth paused to marvel at The First Father's private quarters.

How could Sim live in such clutter? His rock collection infested the room, spilling over the tablerock, hearth, and most of the hard-packed floor. Sure, some were pretty. Elsbeth cherished the pink quartz cluster Sim had given her on the first long winter. But many of these rocks had nothing attractive about them.

A narrow pathway wove between the piles, barely wide enough for her to pass. The shelves bulged with Sim's woodcarvings. At first, he had worked on sections of oak limbs, fashioning walking sticks with notches and fanciful creatures. The one Sim made for Elsbeth had a wooden likeness of their long-deceased friend Benjamin, one of the Pensworthy owls, perched on the top.

In recent years, Sim's craft had extended to musical instruments and bowls shaped from burls of mountain ash. Amid the rock clutter, a small chest stood, complete except for drawer pulls. Was he building furniture now? Maybe it was a Spring Festival gift for someone. Elsbeth hoped, for her.

She cupped her hand over her nose. The cave needed some dried herbs to chase off the musty smell. Sim probably didn't notice the stale odor lurking beneath the twang of wood curls.

Her gaze roamed the room, searching for clues. The peg where Sim normally hung his collection pack was empty. Not good. Sim took that every time he left to dump-dive. His favorite hiking stick, the one with the hawk-head handle was missing too. She peered through the shadows. The bedroll wasn't there either.

"You crazy boy." Elsbeth spotted a smoky quartz cluster resting atop a piece of rolled-up paper. She picked it up, uncurled it, and read Sim's scrawling script.

Dear L. the L.,

Elsbeth twisted her lips at the shortened version of her nickname, Lizard the Lousy. Sim had called her lizard for years—even before they had fled the orphanage in New Haven

City. He added the *lousy* part for the cranky disposition Elsbeth developed during the long underground winters.

She brushed aside her irritation and read on.

Gone for a couple of days. Beat you to the dump this year! Hah!

Elsbeth groaned. Why hadn't Sim left this note on the Common Room board? When she unfurled the scroll, she read his last line. As if he had read her mind.

'Cause you'd go all Lizard the Lousy and try to stop me. That's why.

"You silly goof!"

She flipped over the paper. More writing, in careful block letters.

I'm with him. Grant.

Some of Elsbeth's anxiety eased. If Sim had to jumpstart spring, at least Grant was along. Someone with some sense. She rolled up the little scroll and shoved it into her robe pocket. Should she tell Taproot?

No. The old magician would snarl if she interrupted his preparations for the Spring Festival of Light. Even without his dither and plans for a walkabout, whatever that was.

Slate's dream vision had to be a mistake.

Elsbeth spoke aloud, as if Sim's room held enough magic to send her message to him. "You better bring back something really, *really* good."

Chapter Four

Grant stood at the edge of the landfill, lifting his nose to sniff the air. "Sky to the west promises snow." A line of clouds hung low over the horizon, ominous. A changing wind pushed the evergreens lining the dump pit.

Sim attached his knife and a wind-up flashlight to the carabiner clips on his belt. "Too late in the season for snow. Probably just a little rain. *I* won't melt, will *you*?" He secured his tether line to a small sapling. "Take first dive watch. I'm going in."

"The usual path is blocked."

"I see that." Sim motioned toward a stack of rotted lumber still clotted with snow. "Should be able to enter through there. You worry more than Elsbeth." He patted Grant on the shoulder then walked to the wood pile. In seconds, Sim disappeared and his safety line trailed behind him.

Grant's dark eyes skimmed the area above the landfill, vigilant for predators. He let his vision go slightly off focus, to detect slight movement. It wasn't the things he could readily see that worried him, but those that barely shifted until it was too late to avoid their attack.

Watchers in the woods waited. He was sure of it.

The daylight hours made him twitchy, but dump-diving required some illumination. Little sunlight filtered through the layers of trash. Plus, the rats! No matter how often he entered the mounds of rotting refuse, Grant had a hard time warming up to the vile creatures. They reeked of decay. Then there were the maggots, though the cold temperatures prevented many of them now.

Two buzzards pulled lazy circles in the azure sky. Not such a great hunting day for scavengers. Usually, they appeared in the warm months to feast on rotting carcasses. Nature wasn't acting the ways it should, from what he gathered. The lowlanders and their "science" interrupted the set rhythms of the seasons.

Grant's hand cupped around the acorn-shaped pendant. His spirit-son grew inside, almost ready for the one-spirit magic to bring him into the world. In the past week, the woody acorn had shifted to its crystal form, signaling that the time for the birth grew close. Grant had never anticipated the Spring Festival as he did this year.

Like all youngers, the little one would possess knowledge, so unlike the mewling babies of the lowlanders. As his spirit-father, Grant would teach the child to use his inborn one-spirit's wisdom. Above all the things Grant treasured—his books, maps, the ability to think through most any situation—the small creature growing inside the pendant held the most important spot. He would do anything to protect his spirit-son.

Grant watched the edge of gray clouds approaching from the west. The icy breezes would drive the buzzards to shelter soon.

He and Sim should seek that same shelter.

Something brushed Elsbeth's back. She jerked so hard, she narrowly avoided toppling into a tower of stacked slate.

"Whoa!" Jondu grabbed Elsbeth's arm and steadied her.

Elsbeth held one palm over her heart. "Oh. It's just you."

"Who'd you think it was?" Jondu flicked up one eyebrow. "Maybe an evil rock monster that guards Sim's stuff?"

"Not like I'd take anything." Elsbeth's gaze took in the messy room. "Except that chunk of smoky quartz. Could use it as a book prop." She smiled. "Sim would never miss it, not in this muddle."

Jondu picked up the gemstone: a semi-transparent gray with wispy streaks of black inside, like trapped spider webs. "Soon as I can go topside, I'll pick up a prettier one for you.

I'm good at finding things." She set down the quartz and cocked her head, studying The First Mother. "So . . . what *are* you doing in Sim's cave?"

Might as well talk. Secrets never worked in the clan. They created division. Not good for a small group cooped up together for months at a time.

"Slate had one of his dreams," Elsbeth said. "A bad one. Thought it might be connected to Sim." A wave of fresh panic rippled the tiny hairs on the back of Elsbeth's neck. Not a good sign.

Jondu pursed her lips. She scanned the room for a place to sit. "This is heavy talk. I could use a cup of tonic."

"Doubt you'll find one here."

"Want to go hang at the Hall?"

Elsbeth nodded and they picked their way back to the main tunnel.

"How did you . . .?" Elsbeth started. "Never mind." Silly to think the whole clan didn't know of the seer's dream by now and had figured out she was upset. Just as well. Fear shared equaled fear divided. Elsbeth felt better already.

The clouds hung low and steely, like the curled undercoat of a gray mountain lynx. The weather front inched slowly, so Sim and Grant had stolen a few extra hours to explore one corner of the dump where the trash proved rewarding.

Grant stooped under the weight of his loaded pack. "We'd best try to at least make it beyond Mad Man's Pass and the river before sundown." He patted the birth pod, making sure it rested secure beneath his collar. "I'll feel better as soon as we reach the valley."

The dive had been a success. Sim had found an old wooden sewing box filled with needles and thread, and discarded clothing, enough for several robes. Mari would be ecstatic! Like his, Grant's pack bulged with an unopened can of sweet corn, but they had to leave most of the cache hidden in the woods near the dump. Later, they could bring others to help carry the food back to the clangrounds. Too bad they couldn't use magic to shrink the cans of pinto beans, corn, and soup.

"Wish we had room to take those partial jars of spices, especially the cinnamon." Sim shifted his pack to ease the cramp in one shoulder. "Haven't had cinnamon in years. Good on acorn cakes with honey."

Sim took the lead, but the pack slowed his pace. As they reached the boulder field at the crest of Mad Man's Pass, the sky spit a few flakes of frozen rain. Snow would be better. It crunched underfoot, but didn't cause his feet to slip and slide like the ice.

"Do you want to make camp beneath the boulders?" Grant asked, his eyes searching the clouds. "Maybe we should turn back."

"Let's press on. I'm sure we can make it over the river." A copse of hickory trees marked the opposite shore of Mad Woman River, a spot they often used for night camp.

By the time they reached the riverbank, the frozen rain had switched to snow flurries. The sapling bridge shimmered with a dusty layer.

"Let me go first." Sim cinched his pack strap tight and shifted the weight until it felt more balanced. He took the first steps, testing the surface. Beneath the white frosting, the bark seemed solid, not soggy or slick. "It's not bad at all. A complete klutz could make it across." He finished passage at a fast pace then turned to face Grant.

The sound of clumping steps echoed through the evergreens, rising over the wail of Mad Woman River. Grant and Sim turned toward the noise. Bear? No. This being had two feet and was heavier than most mountain creatures.

Grant's head swung from side to side, searching for cover. The footsteps thudded louder.

"Hurry!" Sim shouted.

Grant protected the birth pendant with one hand, shifted his pack and stepped onto the sapling. When he reached the midpoint, the brush parted behind him. A tall lowlander stepped out. In that second, Grant lost his footing.

Sim watched, his mouth agape. Grant tumbled into the river. The pack dragged with the current, dashing Grant's body against one rock, then another, and another.

The lowlander ran to the edge of the water, took two giant steps, and scooped Grant into his hand.

Sim dove into a patch of pine seedlings. His breath came out in chilled puffs. His hand slipped to the knife scabbard. What chance would a blade less than an inch long have against the lowlander? Judging by his clothing, this man was no ordinary lowlander. Worse. He was a soldier.

Sim watched the man return to the bank and crouch down to study the limp form in his hand. He poked at Grant like Sim often jabbed at ant hills or a rat snake. Anger bubbled up inside Sim. *Stop! that's my first spirit-son!* The furious thought erupted, but he couldn't move.

What was the man doing? The soldier reached into a jacket pocket and pulled out a piece of string, then tied it around Grant. He was roping him like some animal! Before Sim could force himself to do something, *anything*, the lowlander stood. He wrapped Grant's still body in a dark-colored cloth and slipped it inside his jacket.

The man scanned the sky, the same way the clan did to judge the progress of the weather. He crossed the river in five easy steps, without any sort of bridge, and crunched off into the woods.

Sim shucked the heavy pack and scampered back across the sapling bridge to the spot where the lowlander had first stood.

An odd metallic smell twanged his nose. Next to the depressions left by the lowlander's boots, Sim noted two bright red stains against the pristine snow.

Blood.

Chapter Five

When Elsbeth and Jondu entered the Common Hall, Elsbeth spotted her third spirit-daughter Taka-Herb bent over a steaming kettle.

"There you are." Taka-Herb added a pinch of something to the kettle. The pungent scent of steeped medicinal plants blended with the aroma of the turnip stew and acorn bread.

"Valerian root," Jondu identified the herb. "Excellent for settling the nerves."

"Good nose," Taka-Herb said. "I'll make an herbalist of you yet."

Jondu dismissed the comment with a wave. "Only as much as I need to know for my expeditions."

Where had this spirit-child's restlessness come from? Had Elsbeth dreamed of leaving the protection of the peaceful valley as she captured two tears into the birth crystal? Jondu was as different from Elsbeth as Jen, Mari, or Taka-Herb. As unique as shades of emotion could be, she supposed.

Mari and Jen joined the group. Everyone jabbered at once. The voices twirled and blended like the cooking aromas. For a moment, Elsbeth pushed aside her concerns for Sim and Grant—until Slate leaned over and said in a low voice, "Will you tell Taproot about my vision?"

The conversations halted. The clan waited.

Taproot. At his best, the old magician growled until he could go topside. Add to that his frenzied preparations for the Spring Festival and his walkabout.

"No." Elsbeth touched the pendant she wore, a time-smoothed piece of Jen's birth crystal. It rested next to the cherished heart-shaped locket Sim had found dump-diving during the first year. "We won't bother Taproot with this. Sim and Grant will be back in a couple of days." She hoped. "They'll be fine."

"My achy knee tells me another storm is coming," Taka-Herb said. "Not a good time to be tromping around the dump."

"What if they don't make it back?" Slate asked.

"Then Jen and I will go *find* them," Jondu stated with more conviction than Elsbeth could muster.

Jen jumped. Her hand fluttered to the birth crystal.

"What's wrong?" Taka-Herb asked. "You look like you'd been stung by a wild mountain bee."

"I don't know." Jen pulled the crystal from beneath the rim of her robe and turned it in her palm. "It kind of . . . vibrated."

Sim traversed the sapling bridge and dashed toward the spot where he'd dropped the pack. He removed the wind-up flashlight, extra knife, and two bags of dried plums. No way could he travel quickly with the loaded backpack. He stuffed it behind a boulder, not bothering to cover it with leaves and twigs. Nothing would bother a pack without food. Wild creatures didn't appreciate cloth and thread like Mari, and the can offered no enticing hints of its contents.

Snowflakes peppered Sim's head and shoulders. The soldier's boot prints still showed, sunken deep in the first layer of snow. Soon, they would fade and so would the chances of trailing the man.

"Has to be heading to the base." Sim checked the direction of the prints. Without the sun's shadows to discern east from west, Sim relied on other signs. Moss usually shunned the direct sun and grew thicker on the north side of the trees. But that wasn't always the case. Taproot taught that moss could grow most anywhere it found moisture and shade. He watched the movement of the low clouds. Generally, they shifted from west to east. From Mad Man's Pass, the army base was due northwest. Same way the soldier was heading.

He took a moment to consider. Grant was better at weighing options. Sim felt more comfortable with split decisions based on whims.

"Fastest way is cross country, following the soldier's lead." But there was no game trail in case he lost the tracks. Safest path would be back toward the valley then due north on the old dump trail that he used when he went to scrounge the base dumpsters.

"If he's even *going* to the base." Sim frowned. "But with the storm, why wouldn't he be heading toward his kind?"

The thought of facing down soldiers made his heart beat harder. His dad had been the resistance army leader, and his position had gotten him killed. Soldiers had robbed Sim of his lowlander boyhood, his family, and his home. He'd be hanged if one took his first spirit-son too!

The snow shimmered down, heavier now, and the wind picked up to a low whine. No time to stand with his feet ice cold and have a conversation with himself, trying to predict which direction he should chose. Sim shucked his gloves, spit in his left palm, then slapped the moist glob with a finger. Most of the spit splattered to the right, in the same direction of the soldier's path. As good a way as any to figure out how to proceed. He pulled on his gloves and scampered from one boot impression to the next.

Darkness crept into the deep woods sooner than it did on the open game path. After a couple of miles, Sim strained to see the next boot print. The temperature plunged. He snugged his jacket and scarf closer. No way to tell how much farther to the army base. Sim figured Taproot had dragged him and the clan on every switchback in this part of the Emerald Mountains, but he had never walked this tract.

Winter had stripped the hardwoods of foliage, leaving only the evergreens' meager cover. The snowfall dimmed all sound except for the soft shush of his footsteps. Sim looked up. A figure watched from a high limb. Sim imagined how he might look—a tiny wiggling dot against the white. Easy prey, even in the fading light.

A small copse of boulders dotted the hillside ahead. Too risky to continue in the growing gloom. He'd stop for the evening, eat, and sleep. In the first light, he would figure out how to make it to the base. Sim trudged up the incline.

The shadowy form dove from the treetop. Sim broke into a jerky run, his feet sinking into the low snowdrifts. His breath came out ragged, tearing at his burning lungs.

The rush of wings sounded above his head. Sim dropped to his knees and covered his head. He would die and never be able to find Grant! Something heavy landed in front of him.

"Master Sim?" a gravelly voice asked.

Sim peered through a slit between his crossed arms. He sat up. Relief poured over him like one of Taka-Herb's hot tonics. "Kenneth? Is that you?"

"Indeed." Kenneth of the Pensworthy owls swiveled his great round head left, right, then back to regard Sim with golden eyes. The owl's white lower feathers blended with the snow-pocked terrain. Come warmer weather, the earthy shades of his upper body would blend as well with the tree bark. The Pensworthy owls had long been friends of Taproot and the one-spirits, yet Sim respected the night predator's sharp talons. They could snap his body like a withered twig.

"Whatever are you doing out here?" Kenneth asked. "Winter still holds reign. You should be deep underground with the magician and your peers."

"A fact I truly understand . . . now." Sim's shoulders slumped. Cold and worry drained his energy. He could so easily let go, fold himself into a ball, and sleep forever. His eyelids drooped. "I have to keep going. I must."

"Come." Kenneth held out a wing and motioned with a dip of his head. "You will do none of your kind any good if you die."

Sim forced his feet to move until he stood near the great owl. Kenneth folded the wing around Sim and he snugged into the deep down. In moments, his body warmed. Sim recalled Benjamin, the first Pensworthy owl he and Elsbeth had met over fifty years ago. His true friend. The generations that followed were still as trusted, and they all looked somewhat alike. Sim found it easy to think of all of them as clones of Benjamin Pensworthy.

"Hold fast," Kenneth said. Sim grabbed fistfuls of feathers. The owl lifted off, higher and higher, taking Sim with him to a thick thatch of evergreen limbs. He landed then folded his wings back into place over Sim.

Sim curled into the toasty comfort and fell asleep.

Chapter Six

Elsbeth dropped the decanter of hot spring tonic. "Oh, poo!" Soggy herbs hung from her robe hem and fragrant steaming water puddled on the floor at her feet.

"What's the matter with you today, Princess?" Taproot sat on his down sofa. A row of curled maps littered the tablerock in front of him. "That's the third time something in your charge has ended up benefiting the dirt."

"Sorry." She used a wad of old cloth to sop most of the tonic from the earthen floor before it turned to mud. Good thing about caves: spills weren't as much of a problem.

"Maybe I should've asked Mari or Taka-Herb to help with the tonic." Taproot narrowed his eyes and ruffled his beard—better now since he'd given it a much-needed trim. "You're not usually one for clumsiness. What has you so distracted?"

"Oh . . . I . . ." She wanted to tell him. How Sim and Grant had slipped off for an early dump-dive. How they were *still* gone. How each passing minute prickled her stomach like porcupine quills. But Taproot's "dig within" comment still smarted. She'd figure this out. Without his help.

"Is it about the Spring Festival?" He snapped his fingers. "Of course, that's it! This is the first season you won't be a spirit-mother, and it passes along to . . . ?"

"Jen. It passes to Jen."

"Ah." His lips curled up, though all that showed was a slight lifting of the burly mustache. "Bet you're worried about what kind of child she'll produce, eh?"

Elsbeth opened her mouth to reply, but Taproot continued, "The brook wanders, yet doesn't forget its source." He paused. "The ocean gleans its greatness from the streams."

Huh? What did all *that* mean?

Taproot shuffled the maps, frowned, and shuffled again. "Jen's spirit-daughter could be totally different from her. Maybe the child will get the best part of Jen, her willingness to try new things. Besides, Jen does have a certain kindness, a motherly quality. After you get past all the crazy."

Elsbeth plucked long strings of something green and mossy from her robe. When the old magician spoke, a reply wasn't always required. Once, she had fallen asleep while he verbally pondered a point, awakening later to hear him still talking. He never noticed her silence.

"But part of her spirit-mother will live inside of the new younger." Taproot made a jabbing point with one bony finger. "Now, Grant's spirit-son doesn't concern me. Not one whit. That boy started out wiser than most, from the first time he stepped out of the piece of dark stone Sim chose for his birth vessel. Grant *thinks*, yes he does, and all of you, heck maybe even me, could learn a lot from him."

Hope Grant is thinking now, Elsbeth mused. *For both himself and Sim.*

"Festival is only a week away. That is, if this last bit of snappish cold will give up. Never seen such snow so late." Taproot snatched up one yellow section of the rolled paper. "Ah, here it is. Now, if Dell-Fee hasn't moved on, I should be able to find her."

"Is it far?" Elsbeth hoped not. Maybe over a hill or two. Taproot could be there and back in a matter of days, no longer than one of his trips to the bees' hollow.

"Don't know, precisely. This map has no legend. No way to judge true distances."

"Where'd it come from?" Curiosity niggled at her. She crawled onto the sofa beside him and stood on her tiptoes to study the old document.

"I traded for it, with one of the travelers that passed this way before you and Sim came along."

"Wow. It's pretty old."

"Tis. But the mountains and rivers don't change. I should be able to find her cave. *If* she's still alive, and *if* some bear hasn't decided to purloin her home for its den."

"What are these?" Elsbeth pointed to one of the zigzags.

"Mountain ranges." He followed a series of curling lines with the tip of one finger. "And these are rivers or streams." Taproot tapped the map. "This is where we are, in the first valley west of Mad Man's Pass. Here."

"Where's your friend?"

Taproot slid his finger across the paper to a spot marked with a small star. "There."

Judging by the number of lines between *here* and *there*, Elsbeth tried to imagine how long Taproot might be gone.

"I have to leave soon. No telling if I can make it to Dell-Fee's by the fall. Certainly, I can't travel the passes after the first snow."

Wow. He won't be there until the fall. Her pulse stammered. That meant he wouldn't come home until after next year's spring thaw! How would the clan, how would *she*, do without him for so long? "Then you'll come back, right?"

Taproot rolled up the map and stored it in a tube fashioned from curled bark. "Nothing is for certain, Princess."

Sim jerked awake.

Dark. Very dark.

Where was he? In his cave? The foxfire wasn't glowing at all. His foggy brain groped for clues. How could he be so warm if he had allowed the hearth fire to go out?

Then it all came rushing back, one scary scene after another. The frosted log. The crashing steps in the woods. Grant's arms flailing as he fell into the icy swirling water. The soldier.

And the blood.

A slit of light opened above him and he blinked to allow his eyes to adjust.

"Good. You're awake, Master Sim." Kenneth tilted his wing, allowing more of the dim predawn rays to filter down.

Sim pulled himself upward until his head peeked above the top of the great owl's wing. The snow had stopped. Every pine bough held cottony puffs. It was so quiet Sim could hear his own breathing.

"You were hurrying somewhere when I spotted you," Kenneth pointed out. "You never told me. Why are you up here alone?"

Sim recounted the past hours. The owl listened, pivoting his large head from side to side, ever vigilant. Good thing Kenneth was a friend. Sim would hate to be his enemy, or his prey. Sim had witnessed an owl dive for an unsuspecting mouse rustling in the deep grass, using only the light from the stars and his keen hearing. In seconds, the owl dispatched the mouse with one bite to the back of its head. One easy gulp, swallowed whole. The brains, Kenneth once told Sim, were his favorite part.

After the owl heard about the soldier, he said, "I agree. The most reasonable path is in the direction of the lowlander base."

The ground below appeared miles away. The height made Sim a little woozy. "You'd better set me down. I have to get going."

"With your short steps, that valley will be hours, maybe a day, from here. The lowlander has probably reached the base by now. Best I take you. We should get started. I'm not fond of flying in the full daylight."

Sim's mouth dried up. Owl-gliding was Elsbeth's favorite sport, especially on a moonlit night. Jen and Jondu liked it too. They held up their arms and screeched *eeeee!* Then they'd sit for hours afterwards, discussing proper gliding attire, or how they used their toes to grip the down. Sim had only gone owl-gliding twice. Being so far above the treetops scared the beejeebies from him, though he never admitted it to anyone. He stuffed back the rising panic and climbed onto the owl's back, to a spot slightly behind Kenneth's head.

"Let's fly." The words came out before Sim's fright talked him out of it.

Kenneth crouched down, pushed away from the branch, and lifted off. He unfolded massive wings that caught and held the air like billowed sails. Sim squeezed his eyes shut for a beat, forced himself to breathe. The great owl soared through the woods. Tree trunks whooshed by so near Sim could've surely touched them had he trusted himself enough to let one

Rhett DeVane

Dig Within

hand go free. He clung to the thick down until his knuckles blanched white.

Instead of rising farther up, like the hawks, the owl stayed within the cover of the tree canopy, tucking or adjusting the tilt of his wings to avoid collision. Sim's eyes watered in the chilled air. He spotted a lone fox loping through the snowdrifts, a hare dashing for the safety of a pine sapling's lower branches.

The same trip would have taken Sim long hours on the ground, trudging on the switchback game trails ribboning over the hills. Too bad the Pensworthy owls couldn't transport him everywhere. Mari could fashion special owl backpacks to carry dump-dive finds. Eventually, Sim would feel less fear, maybe grow to look forward to owl-gliding

But that would be taking advantage of friendship. Taproot warned about such.

Twice, the owl landed, settled his wings, and studied the woods. His great head swiveled in a half-circle one way, bobbing up and down, then the other, ending with the same bobbing motion. Kenneth's huge yellow eyes missed nothing.

Though his vision was not as keen, Sim watched too. He listened for the sharp *keee-aaar* of a red-tailed hawk or the high-pitched whistle of an eagle. Other birds of prey ruled the daytime skies. Because of their size, the Pensworthy owls were at the top of the food chain. Kenneth appeared formidable, but even he had enemies. Sometimes, other owls. Top on the list: lowlanders. They often trapped and killed owls.

Sim hoped to spot the tracks of the soldier, etched in the white. The night's snowfall had swiped any marks clean.

"The base is over the next pass," Kenneth said. "There's a dead hickory spike near their clearing. We'll stop there."

"Sounds good." Sim's voice came out with more conviction than he felt. If the soldier still had Grant, where would Sim start to search? He had never gone past the row of metal dumpsters where the soldiers discarded their trash. Even then, Sim only scrounged at night when the majority of lowlanders slept. Elsbeth would spit gravel if she knew he went there at all.

From the vantage point atop the dead tree, high above the army base, Sim watched the soldiers. Were they always so active? The area reminded him of an anthill that had been disturbed. Two roads crisscrossed the base, between long rows of barracks and three larger buildings at the spot where the roads intersected. Sim had never seen this much of the military complex. The metal dumpsters where he came to search for castoff supplies and clothing sat at the rear of the buildings, far enough away to hide the scent of garbage. Up until now, that had been close enough.

In their drab camo-print garb, the men looked identical. *Think!* Sim ordered his brain. He searched the brief snapshot memory for something, anything, to help him recall the soldier.

"This is crazy." Sim turned toward Kenneth. "How do I know if the lowlander is down there, or if he still has Grant?"

"We wait," the owl said. His large yellow eyes regarded Sim. "Under cover of darkness, that's when we shall search."

Nighttime. Seemed like it would never come. Every second felt like days. Sim hoped some small detail might point out that one soldier. The individual amidst all the army ants.

"It's like hunting." The owl swiveled his head back toward the base. "The best time to approach the lowlander camp is when the shadows give us the advantage."

Sim had the patrol times memorized. Besides, those army types rarely looked down to his level. They only watched for other lowlanders.

The one place in the Emerald Mountains Sim avoided, except to harvest their intriguing castoffs—the one spot he feared more than any living creature: The army base.

And he had to go down there.

Chapter Seven

Elsbeth slept in fits. The pillow annoyed her the most. She plumped it three times, then slugged it a bunch more. The lumps still pressed against her skin.

Worry and sleep didn't work together. Elsbeth dreamed of her clan scattered like dandelion seeds, tossed by the wind. They called for her, their voices growing farther and farther away. She could do nothing to stop the force carrying them.

The dream faded and another took its place, a twisted tale in which she searched for something, opening door after door to nothing but darkness. Weird. She had not seen a door in over fifty years, not since the orphanage in New Haven City. No need for such here. One-spirits could move from one cave to the next without slabs of wood or steel separating them. Who needed doors when trust existed?

When Elsbeth roused enough to calm the dream fears, the real worries soaked through. She squeezed her eyes shut, willing her brain to stop creating horrible scenes.

Come morning, Sim and Grant would be gone for over twenty-four hours. Either they had landed the dump-dive find of the century, or . . . Her mind went all kinds of crazy places. Sim was brash, sure, but he never stayed gone so long, not unless several of the clan were along. One of the main safety rules: *Past one day, take more to play.* Taproot and his rhymes again, like they couldn't understand without some cutesy saying.

Something shuffled. What now! Her eyes popped open and she waited for her vision to adjust to the low light. No rats down here. Could be one of the many earthworms that often bore holes in her walls on their way to somewhere else.

"Oh, no! Oh, no! Oh, no!" a voice stuttered.

That wasn't an earthworm. For sure. She sat up.

Slate stood by the hearth, shivering.

"What—?"

"It's bad! It's really, really bad!" He rocked and scrubbed his hands up and down his crossed arms.

Elsbeth flipped off the snarled covers and slid her feet into the slippers Mari had knit for her.

Slate mumbled to himself, jiggling from one foot to the other.

Elsbeth approached him slowly. Slate sometimes walked in his sleep. His eyes were open, but that didn't mean he wasn't lost in one of his dream worlds. She touched his face. Cold, with beads of sticky sweat sticking to the skin.

"Slate." Her voice came out soft, gentle. "You're okay. This is Elsbeth. You're in my cave. You're safe."

Slate squeezed his eyes shut then open again. He looked around. "Wha—?"

"Come sit down. I'll make some tea." She herded him to a sitting stone, stoked the fire, then slid a filled kettle onto the hot coals.

"I . . . I . . . I'm sorry." Slate took a deep breath. His shivering calmed a bit.

"I wasn't sleeping much anyway. I could use a cup of tea myself." Elsbeth added two logs to the hearth, then shimmied in place until her backside warmed. "Another dream?"

Slate's head bobbed up, then down.

"Scary one?"

He nodded again. Swallowed hard.

Maybe Slate's second sight wasn't something to envy. At times, sure. Who wouldn't want to see fields of greens or huckleberry shrubs flush with fruit, or to be able to direct a path toward a box of chocolate bars buried beneath piles of trash. But every gift came with a price. *Your strongest fire is also your greatest flaw,* Taproot said. That one, she understood.

Elsbeth offered a slight smile. "Let's wait on our tea. Then tell me about it. If you'd like."

She talked about other things, anything to calm Slate. The upcoming Spring Festival. How much she looked forward to bathing in the stream pool rather than in front of the hearth. About the taste of brook lettuce and dandelion greens, picked fresh and tender. Elsbeth avoided speaking of Taproot and his walkabout.

When the kettle burped steam, she poured two cups and added small cloth bags filled with a blend of dried chamomile and rose hips—both known for their soothing properties. The tea steeped. Then they added honey and sipped.

"Amazing, how this always makes me feel better." Elsbeth cradled the warm cup in her hands. The earthy sweet scent rose up, made her nose as happy as her mouth. Judging by the way Slate's shoulders relaxed, the herbal brew had the same effect on him.

"Something bad has happened," Slate said.

Elsbeth steeled herself. Time to face the unease creeping around them like mountain fog.

"I saw water rushing and twirling. Like it was angry and wanted to wipe away everything in its path."

Were they going to have a flood? Surely the caves were on high enough ground and far enough from the stream. The entrance holes deflected rainfall and snowmelt. *Slate's dreams aren't always exact,* she thought. Sometimes they contained symbols, not reality.

Slate set down his cup. Closed his eyes. "I saw a pack caught on a rock. Torn on one side. The water pushed around it, and it bobbed under, then up. Over and over."

Elsbeth's chest felt cold. She snugged the flannel robe closer.

"Then fast thumping noises. Like heavy footsteps." Slate stamped his feet. "Crunch, crunch, crunch."

A bear? She wondered. No, they hadn't stirred from winter sleep yet.

Slate opened his eyes. Tears glistened in the corners. "Then pain and blackness."

Elsbeth took one last slug of tea and set down her cup. "We have to gather the others."

Elsbeth moved from cave to cave, awakening her spirit-daughters. They trailed behind her to the Common Hall.

Jen jogged beside Elsbeth, peppering her with questions. "What's up? What's going on? Huh? Huh?"

Jondu walked a couple of paces behind, silent. Mari and Taka-Herb yawned, shuffling at the rear of the group.

When they reached the Common Hall, Sim's three spirit-sons waited by the hearth.

"Now, will you tell us?" Jondu asked.

Elsbeth and Slate took turns. Slate relayed the dream messages. Elsbeth echoed her concern.

"So, we go look for them," Jen said. The others nodded agreement.

"Easier to voice than *do*," Elsbeth countered. "The late snowfall has blocked the entrances. No doubt, the same storm is responsible for Sim and Grant's delay."

Jondu planted her feet apart, arms crisscrossed over her chest. "Sim and Grant know how to survive topside. I don't get why you're both flipping out."

Elsbeth tapped her robe above her heart. "It's something I *feel*." She rippled her fingers. "Like a vibration. Haven't you ever done such, Jondu? *Feel* there's danger?"

Jondu moved her head up and down.

The group stood in a circle. No one spoke for a moment. A log snapped in the fire. Gabby hummed low, a habit he had when he was upset.

"I know a way topside," Jondu said in a soft voice. "A deep tunnel made by the moles. It opens beneath two leaning boulders, near the stream, protected from the ice and snow. I followed Sim there one time."

"And I never knew this?" Elsbeth propped her arms on her hips. Sim never kept secrets, not from her!

"He didn't tell," Jondu said. "He was probably afraid someone would go topside too early and get hurt."

Elsbeth snorted. "And it was fine for *him* to do such?" Didn't surprise her, when she stopped to consider it. Not really. "And why didn't *you* tell me?" She swatted the questions aside before Jondu had a chance to answer. "Never mind. Makes no difference."

"I can find them. Remember, I'm good at finding things." Jondu waited for a reply.

"I'll go with you," Jen added. "Better with two of us."

Elsbeth took a deep breath, blew it out. "I should be the one—"

Mari rested one hand on Elsbeth's arm. "No, you should *not*."

Brick cleared his throat. The others turned toward him. "If I may . . . I know I am not the thinker Grant is, nor adventurous like Sim The First Father, but it seems to me, the two most qualified travelers might be the wisest choice. It is this way in my stories. To do otherwise . . . well, it's just foolish." He paused. "The fools who rush in unprepared often end up dead."

Her clan, scattered like dandelion puffs. Wasn't that part of her bad dream? A finger of fear trailed up Elsbeth's spine.

Gabby stopped humming. "We should ask Taproot what to do."

Elsbeth pulled her shoulders back. "No." The solution took shape in her mind. She turned to face Jondu and Jen. "Get your packs." Then to Taka-Herb. "They'll need some small vials of healing herbs. Whatever you think, in case . . . I'll leave that up to you."

She tipped her head toward Mari. "Those down vests you made, and any layers you can add for warmth. Outfit them as warmly as possible."

Mari nodded.

Slate, Gabby, and Brick waited. "Okay, the rest of you—pack up dried fruit and nuts. Enough for a few days."

They watched her, wide-eyed. "Go!" The clan split off, running to the tunnels.

Elsbeth stood alone by the hearth. Was this how her own parents had felt when they asked her to hide behind the hedge when the soldiers came? They couldn't have foreseen the months Elsbeth spent living in alleys, feeding from garbage cans until she landed in the orphanage. Wonder what they would think now, seeing the one-spirit creature she'd become, with her own children.

As her mother had done with her, Elsbeth was sending her daughters into danger, into the unknown. It had to be.

Her spirit ached.

What was her part? She lifted her hands, palms up. Closed her eyes. Chanted the old prayer.

Blessed is the Light. The life and the Light are one. We are the Light. We are one.

Less than an hour later, Elsbeth and the clan assembled again in the Common Hall.

Brick stood back, eyeing the two travelers. "You look like snowballs rolled in dried grass."

True. The worn camouflage material Sim had rescued from some "top secret" dump location the past summer resembled the forest in winter—white background laced with brown branches and bits of dead leaves. Elsbeth sniffed one sleeve. Mari had obviously spent hours slushing the garbage stench from the fabric.

"I think they'll blend in perfectly," Mari said. She snipped a stray thread from Jondu's jacket. "Except for Jen's bright red cap."

"I always wear it. It's my lucky hat." Jen tapped the knit cap with her fingertips.

"This down stuffing is really warm." Jondu tugged at the collar. "We should go."

"We'll walk with you, until you have to step topside," Elsbeth said. Her voice came out squeaky and forced. Emotion threatened to close her throat.

Jondu shook her head. "Nope."

"But—"

Jondu crossed her arms over her chest. "If I show you the hidden exit, you'll be tempted to follow."

Mari touched Elsbeth's arm. "She's right, you know."

Elsbeth took a shaky breath and let it out. "As you wish."

Jondu and Jen hugged all of them, one by one.

"Close your eyes and turn your backs to us." Jondu stood with her thumbs hooked under her pack straps.

"Wait!" Jen dug beneath her collar and slipped the birth crystal pendant over her head. She walked toward Elsbeth and held out her hands. The birth crystal let off a gentle blue glow. "Will you protect her while I'm gone?"

"I . . . I . . ."

"It's wicked cold, topside. I need my spirit-daughter to be safe. Please." Jen pleaded with her eyes.

Elsbeth took the pendant, slipped it over her head, and nestled it beneath her robe. The pendant made a tinkling sound when it bumped against the crystal shard from Jen's birth and the dump-dive locket Sim had given her over fifty years ago.

"Okay, but she's back with you, as soon as you return." Elsbeth noted a faint scent rising from the crystal. Sweet, like the blossoms of wild roses. A flash from her lowlander childhood swept over her: standing in her mother's flower garden, pruning shears in hand, with a basket of roses in yellow, red, and pink hanging from the crook of her arm.

The memory faded, but a hint of rose blooms lingered in her nose. Her anxiety faded a little.

"I'll be at the Spring Festival, one way or the other." Jen gave Elsbeth one last hug. "Keep faith."

Emotions bubbled up again, threatening to choke Elsbeth. She sniffed back tears, squeezed her eyes shut, and turned away.

Moments later, when she spun around, her two spirit-daughters were gone.

Chapter Eight

Jondu veered from the main path and took a smaller trail. The fresh snow snicked beneath her boots. Her toes already ached from the cold.

"Aren't we going to the dump?" Jen asked.

"We'd better check out the passes first." Jondu didn't look back or slow her pace. "Won't take long to take a look from Taproot's watchtower."

In a few minutes, they stood atop the granite cliff. Had Sim and Grant done the same thing before they continued to the landfill? Jondu looked around for signs of other one-spirits. No use. The snow had iced every surface.

"Pretty." Jen shifted her pack. "Never seen it like this."

Jondu had, many times. Only she never let anyone know she left the safety of the clangrounds during the winter. A traveler longed for movement, and she found it impossible to stay cooped up for five long months without venturing outside. She hoped her experience might prove helpful now.

"Mad Man's Pass looks like solid snow pack." Jondu shielded her eyes from the sun's light reflecting from the ice.

"Aw, we can make it through that. Easy."

Jondu turned and studied her spirit-sister. Sure, Jen was older. But not smarter. "I know a deer path we can take. It comes out near the pass. If they've been moving around since the storm, it will make it easier for us."

Jen waved one hand. "Lead on."

They descended through the slit in the granite. Then Jondu turned north. She stopped, searching the forest. "There."

"I don't see anything."

"Believe me. It's there." Jondu worked her way through the thick drifts until she reached a stand of firs. The snow was tamped down, and a narrow path furrowed through the woods.

Once they shifted onto the deer trail, Jen stepped closer behind her. "How'd *you* know about this?"

"Uh . . . um . . ." Jondu hated to lie. "Deer and such usually have certain ways of moving about. They use this one during the warm months, so why not now?" Not exactly a lie. First time Jondu had chanced upon a deer trail slicing the snow, she had reached that conclusion. If Jen had the heart of a traveler, she would've figured the same. Surely, Sim would take the same trail.

Every now and then, roughened divots showed where the deer had pawed and nosed the snow, searching for food. In spite of the serious mission, Jondu enjoyed the trek. To be outside, in the crisp Emerald Mountain air! Free of the sense of dirt pressing down from above and the walls and floors keeping her captive. What if she could live topside all the time? A true traveler like the ones in Taproot's legends would not call any underground cave home. Not for long.

Jondu spotted several rounded impressions, clearly not deer prints. Had to be one-spirit boots. In a spot where the evergreens failed to provide cover, the trail disappeared beneath the layer of fresh snow.

"I want you to walk a straight path toward that tree." Jondu pointed the spot out to Jen. "Then turn around in a circle, standing in one place. Look for footprints."

"What's the point?" Jen rubbed her gloved hands together. "Shouldn't we save our energy?"

Sure, Jondu thought. *Barge ahead and we're bound to come out somewhere. Maybe not the* correct *somewhere.* "When you lose a track, it's important to walk a grid, look for the place where the signs pick up again." Jondu angled her body away from Jen. "Trust me on this, will you?"

Jen puffed out a frosty breath, but followed Jondu's instructions.

Jondu called out, "If you find something, stop and I'll come to you. If not, retrace your steps to where we both started."

Somewhere in the glittery white, Sim and Grant's boot prints would appear again. One-spirits didn't just vanish. Unless something picked them up from above. Something hungry.

Two passes later, Jen whistled and waved her arms. Jondu tromped to her position. Though they were faint in the iced crust, two sets of footprints wove through the pines.

"Good job!" Jondu patted Jen on the back. "See, told you we'd pick up their trail." She blew out a relieved breath.

"But I thought this was just some old deer path? Why did you—"

"Didn't want to get your hopes up, just yet." No need to tell Jen that luck played a part in this.

Jondu took note of another detail. At intervals, someone had snapped the dead ends of tree twigs, one way, then another break close to the first. No animal would do that.

The signal belonged to Grant. Jondu felt sure.

Sim wouldn't take time for such.

The sun dipped lower by the time Jondu and Jen again reached a main trail. The sound of rushing water sounded nearby.

"Won't be too much farther now. I can hear Mad Woman River." Relief settled over Jondu. This trail was wider than the one they had just left, and she knew her way to the dump from here, even if Sim and Grant's prints disappeared. Which they did.

"What if they're not at the dump? What then?" Jen shivered.

"I know they'll be there," Jondu said with more conviction than she felt. "Sim wouldn't go to all this trouble and *not* come home loaded down with dump-dive finds. He's going to catch grief from Elsbeth as it is. If he comes back empty-handed . . ." Jondu paused. "You know how she can be."

Jen nodded.

They walked side by side now. Jen kept up her usual running chatter. Jondu flicked her gaze from the path to the skies, watchful for predators. In a few minutes, they stood at the edge of Mad Woman Gorge.

The fierce water raced below them, jamming against the boulders before roaring downstream. Jondu leaned, turned left, then right. A fallen sapling caught her attention.

"Bet that's where they crossed."

Jen dashed ahead, stopping on the bank before putting one foot onto the trunk.

"Wait!" Jondu ordered. "No way we're going across without a balance line." She took her dump-dive rope from her pack and tied a rock around one end. Swinging the weighted line like a lasso, she whipped the line across the water.

"Drat!" she recoiled the rope. Tried again. And again. Until the rock looped around a low pine bough on the opposite shore. She pulled hard and the rock jammed into the space between the trunk and the limb. "That ought to hold. Now, tie your line around your waist, and loop it over the guide line."

"I don't get it."

"If you slip, the rope will keep you from ending up in the river. I'll pull you out."

"Ah." Jen's eyebrows crimped together. "But, how will you get over?"

"Leave that to me." Jondu wrapped the rope end around her waist and backed up until the line grew taunt. "Watch your footing," she emphasized. "Go *slow*. I mean it!"

Jen inched across and lunged onto the far bank. As soon as Jondu knew her spirit-sister was in the clear, she started across, taking up the slack on the guide rope as she went. Not as secure as if someone held the line for her, but at least she would stand a chance if she fell.

"That was cool, the way you did that," Jen said when Jondu jumped onto the bank beside her. "But how did you know . . . ?"

"When you travel alone, you get creative." Jondu untied her waist rope and jerked the other end from the tree.

"But when . . . ?"

"No time to chit-chat." Jondu stuffed the coiled rope into her pack. "We need to keep moving."

When they reached the landfill, Jondu rested two fingertips between her pursed lips and puffed out three brief whistles. *Twee. Twee. Twee.* Nothing living answered. The wind gave a shushing cry. Jondu shuddered and pulled her scarf close.

"What now?" Jen dropped her pack and rubbed the crest of one shoulder.

The skies to the west hung low with clouds, heavy with the dark promise of another squall. Shafts of weak sun painted strips in the ice frosting the snowdrifts.

Jondu let her vision roam, taking in small details of this edge of the landfill. Except for a few scrabbled lines left by the ever-present dump rats, the last storm had swept the area clean of prints. A flash of blue caught her attention. "There!"

They jogged to a tower of layered boards where a snippet of colored material waved like a tiny flag. "Sim's been here, for sure. He always marks his entrance, especially if he found something good."

Jen turned her head right, then left. "So where are they?"

Easy answer, Jondu thought. Sim and Grant must've doubled back, before the last snowfall. "They're probably at the Common Hall this very moment, all warm and full of food and tonic, making fun of us, up here freezing our tail feathers off."

Then Jondu spotted something else. She walked toward a small clearing, surrounded by a semi-circle of boulders. The spot, she knew well. She and the one-spirits had made overnight camp here many times when the dump-dive treasures were too good to leave.

The remains of a large campfire rested beneath an overhanging slab of granite. Jondu kicked one charred limb aside and held her hand above the crumbled embers. Her mind whirred into gear. A lifeless lowlander fire. No Sim. No Grant. Her spirit iced cold. "We have to head back."

Jen held up both hands. "It's going to be dark soon. Shouldn't we—?"

Jondu pulled her pack close. "If we have to stop, I'll find a place for us to make camp. C'mon. Now!" She moved down the path as fast as the glazed rocks would allow. Once they rejoined the main trail, she stopped at regular intervals to study pieces of bent twigs. Jondu looked up and spotted jagged, torn branches high above their heads. The level of a lowlander's passage. Not placed on purpose to mark a trail. The spit dried in her mouth.

Without speaking, Jondu increased her pace. Jen shuffled behind, firing off questions and grumbling when Jondu failed to answer.

When they reached Mad Woman Gorge, Jondu noticed something she hadn't seen when they passed by on the way to the landfill: a glob of snow marbled with dark red. She crouched, held the colored ice crystals to her nose. Sniffed. She pawed the snow to reveal a deeper stain, this one much larger.

An ominous feeling crept over Jondu, worsening by the moment. "Change of plans. No guide rope this time. Watch and do exactly as I do."

Before Jen could answer, Jondu crawled on and straddled the sapling, placing both hands on the trunk in front of her. She butt-hopped forward, keeping her thighs clamped around the tree.

In the creek below, a ribbon of material bobbed in the current. Jondu stopped. She broke off a limb and lay down on the log. With one arm, she hugged the sapling. With the other, she used the limb to jab the fabric until it broke free. She lifted the cloth long enough to identify it, then dropped it back into the swirling water where it joined the debris rushing toward the falls.

As soon as Jondu reached the far bank, Jen followed. She slid to the end of the sapling and stood on the rock. "Why did you stop in the middle? What was that thing you pulled up?"

"Be quiet. Please." Jondu whipped her head from left to right. *C'mon Grant. You've left me signs all along. Don't stop now!*

The only depressions in the snow: those same large-ridged boot prints. Had to be something more, something she was missing. There! She dashed toward a small boulder, knelt, and tugged at the strap of a backpack until it slid out.

Jen ran and stood beside her. Her jagged breath came out in frosted clouds. "Isn't that—"

"Sim's pack."

Jondu's gaze darted across the surrounding snow. Only one faint set of prints followed the tree line, heading in the same direction as the boot prints. Why only *one* set? Sim would never leave his filled pack behind. Unless . . .

Jondu snapped to her feet. Flicked a quick glance to the growly gray clouds. "We have to follow those boot prints."

When Jondu could no longer see any impressions hashing the snow, she stopped. "We'll have to walk again at dawn."

The last meager sunlight struggled through the barren trees. No shadows. No moon or starlight. No caves or anywhere to take cover.

"What'll we do?" Jen asked.

"Gather as many branches as you can." Jondu shucked her pack and leaned it against a tree. "Walk a grid, like we did before, and return in your same steps." She shook one finger. "Don't go too far."

Jen dropped her pack at the base of the same large pine and grumbled, but did as she was told. Jondu aimed in the opposite direction and walked. By the time they had dragged back a pile of brush, Jondu could barely make out the outlines of the trees.

Jen scrubbed her hands over her crossed arms. "It's fr-fr-freezing!"

Jondu positioned the two packs about a foot apart, then balanced two fat limbs between them. She stacked branches in a circle around the packs, using the first two for support. "Do like this."

"Wha—?"

"No time to explain. Just do it!" Jondu immediately regretted her harsh words. "Hey, sorry. Just . . . please do it."

The limbs formed a thick lattice above the packs, with a little space left for a door. "Now, grab handfuls of snow and pack them on top."

They worked by feel until the small dome was covered.

"It's like a little cave," Jen said.

The call of an owl rang through the forest. *Woo-ooo-ooo! Woo-ooo-ooo-ooo!* One of the Pensworthy owls, Jondu hoped. Should she answer?

No. If it was not a friend, the cry would summon winged death. Claws swooping down with no sound. Jondu shivered.

"You climb in first," Jondu whispered.

She heard Jen's crunching movements, then felt her way into the makeshift storm shelter and tugged a matted clump of brush and packed snow over the entrance hole.

They huddled together with the packs on either side.

"Not bad," Jen said. "Warmer than outside, for sure."

Nothing was *for sure*. If they made it through the night. If they didn't freeze into matching one-spirit sickles. If that storm didn't hit. If they could still follow those prints and find Sim and Grant.

If. Jondu kept her worries to herself. *I hate that word.*

Chapter Nine

"My pack sure would come in handy right about now," Sim said. He thought about the things he didn't have—his rope tether, basic first aid supplies, extra food. At least he had his flashlight and knife.

"Owls never carry packs," Kenneth stated. "And we seem to do quite well."

Sim smiled, in spite of the churning in his stomach. During the long day, loaded trucks had left the complex in a steady stream, and jeeps came and went. What was going on? Nothing good, if the army was involved. With the growing darkness, the base had settled into relative calm.

"I'll take you down to the shadowed spot behind the last building." Kenneth indicated the direction with a tilt of his head. "There isn't an outside light there, and the search beams don't cross that area."

Sim had been so busy worrying that he hadn't taken into account the lights streaking across the grounds. Never had to concern himself with that before, since the base dumpsters occupied an area away from the barracks. Nights in the forest were easy, compared to being around lowlanders and all of their unnatural light. The owls hunted at night, but many in this part of the Emerald Mountains were either related to the Pensworthy clan, or close enough to honor the ban on killing, and eating, one-spirits.

When Sim made a move to crawl into his owl-gliding position, Kenneth twitched one wing. "Best if I pick you up with my talons. I can drop you easily and fly off before anyone takes note." The owl blinked. "No reason to appear so alarmed, Master Sim. I can hook onto your jacket and never touch your skin."

Sim swallowed around a dry lump.

"Make sure your jacket is secure," Kenneth instructed. "I will swoop down to pick you up."

Sim loved excitement, but being snatched from a treetop by an owl's talons? Made him want to crawl into a deeper hole than the one where he lived. Maybe never, ever come out. What choice did he have?

"Keep your legs tucked to your chest, like I carry mine while I'm in flight. When I set you down, roll. You won't get hurt. Clear?"

"Um . . . okay."

Kenneth lifted from the branch and disappeared into the night. Sim checked to make certain his jacket was buttoned and folded himself into a ball, covering his head with his arms. Sim felt himself snatched up. The wind curled around him. Good thing the shadows hid the ground. It was a long way to tumble, but Sim couldn't pick out details.

Kenneth's wings made no sound. The wispy edges snuffled the rush of air moving across the feathers. No wonder the owl was such a deadly predator. A mouse would be jerked upward before it had a chance to squeak.

Death dropping from the sky.

Sim held his legs tucked tight. They passed over the treetops at the periphery of the base. The owl threaded between the buildings, avoiding the searchlights' beams. Lower, lower, until Sim could smell the snow-damp ground. A couple of inches, then Kenneth's talons released their hold. Sim hit with a dull thud and rolled over and over in the fresh snowfall.

He sat up and blinked. Snow clotted on his clothes. He patted his arms and legs. Nothing bleeding or hanging at a strange angle.

What a ride! He might learn to love flying after all.

He watched a soldier pass beneath the pool of dim light in front of one of the barracks. The army men looked alike in those uniforms—as if they were trying to be copies of each other. This one had short, stubby, yellow hair. Reminded Sim of a porcupine, the way it stuck straight up on top.

Was this quill-haired lowlander the one who had taken Grant?

Sim took a deep breath and stood, forcing himself to pull back his shoulders. Taproot always said, "Act brave and you'll be brave."

Tell that to my stomach, he thought.

Careful to stay within the shadows, Sim tailed the soldier. The man swung his left arm more than the right, and the right elbow crooked out from his body at a strange angle, as if someone had snapped it off and put it back sideways. The soldier picked up his pace. Though Sim struggled to keep up, he fell behind. He reached the cross street where the man had taken a left turn. Quill-hair had disappeared.

Sim puffed out a breath. Nothing to do but choose a building and figure a way to get inside. He listened. No footfall. No lowlander talk. He dashed across the street, dodging the trail of the overhead beam slicing the air above his head.

Crouched in the darkness, he pondered. Where to start? Grant would come up with some precise fashion for a search. Not willy-nilly. Sim pinched his lips tight, thinking about how many times his spirit-son had accused him of skipping from one thing to the next. Even at the dump, Grant worked a well-planned grid. Sim picked his direction based on whim.

Like the soldiers' uniforms, the buildings looked identical. This one seemed as good a place to start as any. Sim pulled out the wind-up light, gave the handle a few turns, and then inched along the foundation. His eyes darted from the bottom of the steel siding to his surroundings and back. Unless a lowlander stood nearby, his tiny light could go undetected.

He worked the periphery and spotted no gaps large enough to pass through. Now what? A pipe led from the ground to the roof at one corner. Back in New Haven City, the buildings had pipes and vents, sometimes chimneys, breaking through the roof. Possibly a way inside?

Sim considered. If he could scale a bee hollow tree, surely he could climb the pipe. The first two tries, his feet slid on the metal and he made no progress. He slipped off his boots, stuffed the socks inside, tied the shoelaces together, and suspended the lashed boots from his neck. His lips pinched together when his skin touched the chilled pipe. It took three tries, but he finally inched his way upward and stood on the roof. His feet burned. Not good. Frostbite could nip off toes. Sim took a moment to rub both feet between his hands and catch his breath then pulled on his sock and boots. The pipe he had ascended ended, spilling forth a spray of thick wires. No passage into the building through that one.

A conical cap covered the next pipe he noticed. The air around it smelled like the stench from the necessary rooms. Sim backed away. No way would he crawl down some forbidding hole smelling of lowlander waste. He moved on. On the opposite side of the roof, he inspected yet another pipe, smaller, but not as stinky.

One problem. His dump-dive rope was in his pack, stuffed under a rock beside Mad Woman River. Sim unbuttoned his coat and removed his shirt. Good thing he had his knife, and it was always sharp. He hacked and ripped the shirt into long thin strips and tied them together. Mari would thump him on the head for destroying a perfectly good piece of clothing. He'd worry about that later. He donned his jacket next to bare skin.

One end of the rope, he looped around the pipe. The other, he fastened around his waist. Sim tugged to make sure the makeshift tether would hold his weight. Good as any dump-dive rope. He wiggled under the metal cap and rappelled down the inside of the tube, using one hand wrapped around the rope as a brake. The scent of stale oil hummed in his nose, a lowlander odor he recognized from dump-dive finds. Had to be some kind of cook fire vent. Hope the lowlander on the other end wasn't hungry. If hot air seared up this pipe, he'd be charred like a stump struck by lightning.

A dim light glowed at the end of the vertical tunnel, and Sim used his hands against the rope to slow his pace. He dropped into a wooden box of some sort. Sim foraged in his memory. A cabinet? Had to be. The wind-up light held enough charge for him to do a quick search. Amber and clear bottles, some square containers. The scent of strange herbs and spices. Sim closed his eyes, willing his mind to recall details of his lowlander life, so many years in the past. A military slang phrase popped into his mind: *chow hall*. His father's barrack had a cabinet like this, over a hot surface used for preparing meals. As he suspected, the pipe he had slipped down was a vent for cooking odors.

Sim wove past jars and canisters to another opening, the source of the faint light.

Ah, this is where the vent pulls out the stale air. On the other side of a strange contraption, a screen covered the opening. In the dim light below, Sim finally spotted the interior of the building. A way in! He noodled his body between wires and curved things that looked like stiff white daisy petals stuck to a hard center, then pushed against the mesh. Clips held it on two corners, but one side moved enough for him to wiggle through the gap. He untied the cloth rope after he landed on the stove surface and left it swinging. Escape route. Might need one.

The room looked at once familiar and foreign. Long counters. Objects lined up against the wall. Large shiny spoons, forks, and rows of dented pots hung from overhead racks. A cube of wood held knives. Only the worn handles showed. The business ends hid, sunk deep in the thick block.

Sim swung his head to take in the rest of the room. Stacks of dishes and drinking containers. A tower of dingy towels. In one corner, a large silver box hummed low, like bees in a hollow stump. The scent of seared meat hung in the room like a restless ghoul. Sim shivered.

The sticky tang of blended lowlander sweat irked him. Had his father smelled that way, too? Sim had been twelve years old the last time he saw the man. His father's scent, like the memory of his voice, had long faded. The scientists who came to the glen every couple of years didn't have this odor. It reeked of fear and anger and dark things.

Sim shoved aside thoughts of his father. No time for such. He had been dump-diving for half a century, since that first spring. If he could meander through rotting meat ripe with maggots, he could stand lowlander stench.

Anything to find his spirit-son.

Nearly an hour later, Sim crawled onto the hut's ice-slick roof and sucked in clean air. The scents of lowlanders lingered in his nose. Though he seldom used Taproot's special anti-stink goo, he slipped the tiny jar from his inside jacket pocket and swiped a glob above his lips. A blend of camphor and rosemary filled his nostrils. Even the dump in high summer smelled better than the metal houses of the soldiers.

Despair threatened to shut Sim down. He'd only covered five buildings. At this rate, it would take at least two nights to check the army base. He peered toward the skies. Without a moon to tell him how many hours remained of darkness, he had no way to judge how much longer he might search. Cloud cover blanched even the meager starlight. Other than the dim base lamps and the sweep of the search beam, the area was one dismal void.

A form dropped beside him. Sim jumped so hard, his feet slipped on the ice. He grabbed the pipe to regain balance. "Oh, it's just you."

"Who else?" Kenneth settled his wings. "Not much besides us moving around tonight."

"Good thing." Sim blew out a breath and reached into his coat for a sliver of dried plum. He chewed. True, few soldiers occupied the base. Where had they gone? Off killing people, doing things soldiers do, Sim supposed. "This is taking more time than I expected."

"Why don't I transport you from one roof to the next? I can observe from the watch tree until I see your head pop up from the pipe. Will that help?"

Why couldn't he have thought of that? *I'm the bold adventurer. The one who starts quests!* Sim groused to himself. *It's not my job to think!* No, that was Grant's job. "Sure. Good idea."

At least Kenneth didn't offer a smarty reply. Sim stuffed down the fear threatening to close his throat. He took a quick swig of spring water from his pouch then tucked the water container beneath his clothing. "I'll wave my muffler when I'm ready for you to take me to the next building. Let's go."

Sim hunkered down. The owl lifted and speared his jacket with sharp talons. In less time than it would've taken Sim to slide down the gutter to the ground, he stood atop the next building. Kenneth disappeared into the gray.

The next five huts proved more of the same. Nothing to tell who lived there, like rocks or drawings. Even some of Elsbeth's dried flowers would be good. Sim felt a little sorry for the lowlanders. How would it be, to look the same, dress the same, act the same? Like nobody mattered. Only one hut held a soldier, and he slept in his narrow cot bundled beneath a moss green blanket, snorting out honks of air.

No sign of Grant. Sim's spirit shriveled.

Chapter Ten

"Bah!" Taproot slammed his hand down on the tablerock. The lemongrass tea in his mug jiggled. "The one spring I want to go walkabout and we have not one, but *two*, late storms!"

The honey cake Elsbeth had barely managed to swallow churned in her stomach.

"Sure, I can shove my way from the hollow. Easy-peasy." The old magician picked up a now-cold pancake and gnawed on one side, frowned, and thumped it back on the plate. "The recent storm cast a good two feet of fresh powder on top of that last soft layer. It's a set-up for avalanches, given the heavy amount of snow we've had this winter." He slumped into a cushion. "Guess I'm not going anywhere soon. Postpones our Spring Festival too."

Elsbeth nodded.

"Ah, well. What's a couple of weeks, more or less, when I haven't seen my old friend Dell-Fee in decades."

When Elsbeth didn't reply, Taproot continued, "We have to do our spring chores too. Can't get that done until the weather lets up."

Elsbeth's lip snarled at one corner. Spring chores. She thought of the most disgusting one: cleaning out the necessary rooms. Ugh! They'd have to dig five months of soiled dirt from the refuse holes and cart the buckets topside to a location far from their fresh water source. Left to her and the other one-spirits, that bad dirt could stay put. But Taproot insisted on the yearly spring cleanout. That, or they would have to dig fresh necessary rooms and tunnels every couple of years.

Taproot refilled their cups and tilted his head, studying Elsbeth. "What's up, Princess?"

"Huh?"

"Don't play dumb with me. I've been around you enough to know something's amiss. You're usually yammering away so hard I can barely get a word wedged between." He pointed a finger at her and drew a circle in the air. "This is more than your usual winter doldrums."

Under Taproot's stern scrutiny, Elsbeth caved. "I'm . . . worried."

"Spill it." Taproot flicked one eyebrow up and down. "Burdens shared are burdens halved."

Elsbeth inhaled and blew out a breath. At least this riddle made sense. Beyond being her mountain life teacher and magic mentor, Taproot was a friend. She did not like keeping anything from him, large or small. Jen's spirit-daughter crystal tapped against her chest, one more reminder of her problems. "I think I might have made a bad decision."

"If I had a chocolate bar for every wrong choice I've made over the years, we could eat for the rest of our lives." He used his pointy finger to jab upward. "Reminds me. I have a couple of pieces left." He stood and scurried across the room, returning with a battered metal tin. Inside rested two wrapped pieces of dark chocolate. Taproot handed one to Elsbeth and palmed the other. A special treat, since chocolate came only from a rare dump-dive find, or sometimes from the scientists who frequented the valley.

Elsbeth nipped pieces of the chocolate and relayed the events of the past few days. The confection coated her tongue and made her words sweeter, she figured. As she spoke, Taproot's expression darkened. He leaned forward, resting his elbows on his knees. "And it's been four days since Sim and Grant left, and two since Jondu and Jen went to search?"

Elsbeth nodded.

"Why didn't you come to me?" Taproot held both hands out, palms up.

She couldn't meet his gaze. "Because you said I should dig within and figure things out for myself." She picked at one jagged fingernail until it ripped. "And you were *so* busy, getting ready to leave for your walk around or whatever . . ."

Taproot leaned down until he was at her eye level. "While I admire your gumption, Princess, I am never too busy when it's a matter of life and *death*." The word hung in the air between them, dripping menace. Elsbeth swallowed. Her throat felt as if it was paved with rows of Sim's pebbles instead of the silky chocolate.

"Looks like I'll be going topside today after all." Taproot chomped the last of his chocolate nugget and stood. Since the other packs bulged with provisions for his long trip, he pulled out a ratty dump-dive bag. Within minutes, he had shoved in dried fruit, nuts, and other supplies. He grabbed a walking stick and a small camp ax. "Whatever you do, don't let any of the others leave the clangrounds. Four of you wandering around in the deep snow are enough." Taproot pulled on a rainbow-colored knitted cap, Mari's gift from the past Fall Festival.

Elsbeth jumped up. "I'm going."

"Now, Princess . . . I don't." Taproot stopped.

If Elsbeth's expression was as determined as she felt, the old magician would get the message. Nobody would notice her absence. Sometimes, Elsbeth went a couple of days without joining the clan in the Common Hall. They'd figure she was in one of her Lizard the Lousy moods.

"Okay." Taproot snatched up his cup and took one long drink. "Put on warm clothes. Grab your pack. Meet me at the hollow tree exit." Bits of chocolate clung to his beard. "And I mean it about the others. Nobody leaves here but us. Clear?"

Sim stood on the roof of a long building similar to the others but twice the size. Lights shone from a couple of the windows. He didn't note any movement.

"Last hut, this row," Kenneth said. "Might think about stopping after. The sun is teasing the horizon."

"Just this one. Then we'll move to the watch tree." Sim took a long swig of water from his pouch. He hated to halt the search, but daytime was too risky. The few lowlanders on base would be up soon, moving around. Weariness washed over Sim. His back and legs ached. Rope burns crisscrossed his palms like angry red tattoos. Some sleep would be nice.

"I'm sure this won't take me long." Sim recapped the water pouch and swiped the dribble from his lips. "I have this search thing down. Ten minutes, tops."

Kenneth took off. Sim could make out the owl's outline when he landed on the watch tree. Better make this search a quick one. The darkness lifted more with each passing minute.

Sim fastened the rope and descended the pipe. Shortly, he stood on yet another counter. The scent of this barrack differed. Mixed with the lowlander stench was an odd blend of odors Sim couldn't identify. He pinched his nostrils shut until he could swipe Taproot's salve beneath his nose. Even then, the air burned his eyes.

He rappelled down the lower cabinet and landed on the floor. As before, he left the escape rope hanging.

Nothing prepared him for what lay in the next room.

The stinging rank odor of decay knifed Sim's nose at the same instant he took in long rows of cots, pushed close together. Some were empty, their sheets pulled taut. Others held lowlanders.

Sim crouched beneath a chair, trying to understand the scene. Why were all the lowlanders so still, some with sheets covering their faces, while others seemed to be asleep?

Every now and then, one would moan or cry out. Shiny metal rods stood like sentinels at the head of each bed. A few held bags suspended from hooks. Long tubes snaked from the bags to the lowlanders.

The room stirred a deep memory. Same large room. Rows of cots.

Is this an orphanage, like Westside House? Sim wondered. That place where he and Elsbeth had met, where they lived until they fled for the Emerald Mountains.

But these were full-grown lowlanders, not children cast aside by war.

Sim's curiosity nudged him. He jetted from beneath the chair, careful at first to hide beneath the cots as he studied the reclining lowlanders. He became bold, standing for long minutes beside the beds, taking in the yellowed, waxy skin. The odor of sickness.

A hospital! Had to be it. Made sense why these few weren't with the others who had sped off in the loaded trucks.

Sim scaled one cot's frame and sat on the sheet, watching a dark-haired lowlander. Deep smudges colored the skin beneath his eyes, and his breath came out in ragged spasms followed by long periods when his chest didn't move at all.

Death fascinated Sim. He'd often observed animals in those final minutes. Watched their bodies twitch until they became still and the warmth left them. *Passing into the Light* was what Taproot called it. What light, and where did they go when they went over there? Did it hurt? What part of them left, exactly? Was it like the vapor rising off the water's surface on a cool morning?

Something fell over him, ringing the sheet at his feet. Sim jumped up and hit his head against a dome made from wire mesh. His hands flitted around the cage, testing for a place to escape.

"Gotcha!" A deep voice said.

Jondu opened her eyes. Someone snuggled beside her, mumbling in sleep. Where was she? Then she remembered and was surprised she and Jen were still alive. Only she'd never admit such thoughts to Jen.

Mmmmm. Jen moaned and shifted next to her. "I can't move my legs."

"It's because we've been cramped up for so long. We should get going. I think the sun's up." Jondu pushed against the twig door, expecting it to shift easily. Nothing moved. "Put your feet next to mine and help me."

Jen grimaced, forcing her legs to straighten. She tilted back and rested her boots next to Jondu's.

"On the count of three . . . one . . . two . . . three!" Jondu shoved as hard as her stiff legs would allow. The twig thatch didn't budge.

Jen's breath came out in frosted puffs. "We're trapped!"

"Smooth yourself down, Jen. No need to go all rabid raccoon." Jondu repositioned her feet. "Try again."

They kicked, pushed, grunted. Four bursts later, the laced twigs shifted a few inches.

"I don't see the outside," Jen said. "Just white."

Way to state the obvious, Jondu thought. Lack of food and her cold achy joints brought out the cranky in her. She reeled in her mood and forced her voice to come out calm. "It must've been a heavy snowfall last night. We're probably beneath a little drift."

"What'll we do now?" Jen's lips quivered, rimmed in purple-blue.

We have to move soon or we won't be moving at all. Jondu kept the frightening truth to herself. She tugged at her pack until she could reach the top opening, then extracted a tin can and lid she used for camp dishes. "Use these. Dig!"

Jondu tore into the snow barrier. She wasn't going to die. Not now. Not like this, buried beneath a house of twigs and ice. How absurd. They dug and hurled clots of snow behind them.

"Stop." Jondu twisted her body enough to position one foot over the excavated hole. On the third kick, the crust flaked away, revealing a shaft of weak morning light.

Jen joined and they both kicked until the hole widened enough for them to crawl out and wrestle their packs through.

The forest floor lay beneath a thick blanket of powdery snow. Jondu scanned a circle around their makeshift camp. The storm had cloaked the boot prints, as if no lowlander had ever passed this way. The milky sunlight provided no shadows. Hard to tell which way to go. Overhead, the evergreen canopy shielded the sky. Below, familiar landmarks hid beneath the ice.

"What do we do?" Jen's voice shook as hard as her body.

"Change perspective." Jondu took the dump-dive rope from her pack and looped it around her waist and the first branch over her head.

"Are you—?"

"I have to go above the tree line, to tell where we are and which direction to head." If she could climb a rock wall or a bee hollow, she could manage this. The limbs and needles might prove bothersome. Jondu inched up the trunk, moving the safety rope up one branch at a time, the way Taproot had taught her. "Keep an eye out for hawks," she called back to Jen.

Jondu scaled the trunk. The pine needles pricked her chapped face. She coached herself with every inch she ascended. Don't think about the ground. Don't think about how high up you are or the wind swaying this tree. Or how very long this will take to reach the top. Breathe. Easy. Breathe. Easy.

The last few feet proved the most difficult, with fewer branches to grasp. Jondu finally reached the limb cluster at the tree's apex. With her feet snugged as close to the trunk as possible, she pivoted to take in the view. The boulder field near the landfill showed to her right side, but trees hid all but one curvy ribbon of Mad Woman River. She took note of the notched top of Sleeping Bear Mountain. That meant the army base rested a little shy of her left shoulder, in the valley. She scanned the distance for something, anything she might use to keep them on track.

Jondu smiled. There! A dead ash tree, full of woodpecker holes. Before that, she noted a copse of boulders: three, shaped like anthills. A fourth stone leaned over the top, forming a rock arch. Good enough. She memorized her new landmarks.

The descent proved easier than the ascent. If she had to climb another tree later on, she could. Elsbeth and Taproot would be proud.

Jen stamped her boots, hugging herself. "Glad you're back down. Something big is moving over there. Did you hear that weird call?"

"Yes. Didn't sound like the hawks at the landfill or one of the Pensworthy owls." Jondu pulled on her pack and snapped the belt. A hard day's travel lay ahead and most likely well into the night. "Doesn't matter. We can't stay here."

Chapter Eleven

Elsbeth snuggled deep into the muffler wrapped around Taproot's neck. The going was slow, even with the odd contraptions the mountain man had strapped beneath his boots. Her size allowed her to hitch a ride. She'd never manage in snow deeper than her height.

All four of her missing clan members had to be okay. They *had* to! "What are those wacky things on your feet?" Elsbeth continued with a constant line of chatter to trick her mind from worry.

"Snow shoes, Princess."

"Ah." She had noticed the petal-shaped wooden loops leaning against one wall of Taproot's library, but figured them to be some kind of herbal drying racks. During the long, dull winter days, she pondered on such and wished to ask, but Taproot sealed himself off for most of the cold season, professing to need a break from interaction.

By the time each spring arrived, Elsbeth's questions slipped her mind when the clan dove into festival preparations. Then summer came with its long days filled with gathering and preserving food, and fall with the harvest of acorns and other nuts. Then the Fall Festival and . . . Elsbeth sighed. Winter again.

"Wish I had a pair of those snow shoes in my size," Elsbeth said.

"They are heavy. Would only slow you down. We don't have the luxury of turning this into a stroll."

His words came out so clipped, Elsbeth decided to seal her lips and help him watch for signs of the others. A large cat crossed the path a few feet from them. Taproot halted. The animal stared at them for a couple of seconds then bounded off into the woods.

"Emerald Mountain lynx. A sight you don't often see." Taproot resumed walking. "They're elusive critters."

And probably would eat a one-spirit in an easy bite. Elsbeth shivered and hunkered lower into Taproot's muffler.

By the time they reached Mad Woman Gorge, the afternoon light filtered through the snow-tipped evergreens, turning the ice crystals into sparkly rainbows.

"Now, where would they gain passage across?" Taproot pondered aloud. He swung his head right, then left. "Ah, there." He made his way toward a place where a toppled sapling spanned the river. He searched the ground.

"No prints, but these drifts cover any signs." Taproot unlashed the snowshoes, hooked them onto the back of his pack, and bounced one foot on the sapling. "It should support me. Better than getting wet feet. Hang on."

The mountain man held both arms out like those tightrope walkers he had often mimed in the old tales from his life with the lowlander circus. Ten steps took them to the opposite side. He lashed on the snowshoes again. Glanced around for prints.

"Look." Elsbeth pointed to a series of broken twigs low to the ground, at the level a one-spirit would travel. "Grant always does that when he marks a trail."

"Good eyes, Princess." Taproot squinted into the distance. "I'll just bet those four are by the landfill, tucked beneath some rock, eating dried plums and chortling about how all of us might be worried about their crazy selves."

The boulder field at the edge of the landfill showed in the distance. Elsbeth's spirit lifted.

Jondu took a step and sunk up to her shoulders. Jen held out one hand and tugged until Jondu pulled free.

"We'll never be able to walk across this," Jen said.

"For an adventurer, you sure are a downer." Jondu took off her pack and mashed it as flat as possible. "Follow my lead." She lay down, resting her belly on the pack, then used her feet to push herself along. Jen huffed, but did the same.

The two sledded across the snow until Jondu signaled them to stop next to a pine sapling.

"This is okay for short distances, but we need a way to cover a lot of ground, up *and* down hills." Jondu used one of Sim's flint knife blades to saw through several pine boughs.

"What are you going to do with those?"

"Watch." Jondu pulled out a ball of twine, grateful she had remembered to add it to the pack. She lashed the cut end of three short branches together, with the needle clumps forming a fan on the other end. Then she made three more sets. Jen stood, a slight frown painting her features.

Jondu stored the leftover twine and her knife, and placed two of the bound clumps in front of Jen. "Put your boots here, and here."

"But, I don't get—"

"Just do it, please."

Jen stepped onto the spots where Jondu indicated. Then Jondu used two ends of the twine to secure the limbs to Jen's boots. Jondu tied the other two bound clumps to the bottom of her own boots.

"What are these things?" When Jen lifted one foot, the fanned clump followed. "I feel like a duck."

"Walk a couple of steps." When Jen didn't move, Jondu added, "Go ahead. Try."

Jen managed a few wobbly shuffles, nearly falling at first. She got the hang of lifting her feet higher than normal, almost marching. "Hey, they work!"

"Sure they do. If you watch the ducks walking in the mud sludge next to the stream, they don't sink. It's the way their feet are shaped."

Jondu smiled. All of those times she'd slipped topside to observe the animals and mimic their behavior had finally paid off. If she could survive in this kind of forbidding terrain, she could travel anywhere, at any time of year! She reached into her pack and fished around for her dried plums. Only two strips left. Bad planning there. She chewed on one strip. They'd have to forage beneath the snow for deer berries. Hope to find some.

Jondu high-stepped to catch up with Jen and handed her the other piece of dried plum. She got her bearings, then turned forty-five degrees to the left and took the lead.

"**That cackle** sound is close." Jondu held out one hand. "Stop."

She and Jen had traveled the switchbacks across one large hillock, jumped over a small brook, and now stood at the edge of a clearing. The anthill-shaped boulders Jondu used as a landmark rested at the far corner of the meadow beneath a copse of skeletal hickory trees.

She'd seen many such fields on her solitary excursions. In the spring and early summer, soft grasses and wildflowers would paint the ground white, yellow, lime green, and pink. Hard to believe their seeds rested beneath the layers of white.

A large bird flew from the top of an evergreen, its wings spread straight out. Jondu jerked Jen by the arm and they dove beneath a thatch of dead briars. The owl swooped lower, lower, with legs extended. One burst sent the snow crust flying. The owl lifted away, a struggling creature clasped in its talons. When the bird reached a high barren limb, it landed and cackled. The captive creature emitted a screech. In one swift movement, the owl picked up the limp catch with its beak and swallowed the creature whole. Probably a vole. The small rodents tunneled beneath the snow, doing whatever voles do. Until an owl made them into a quick meal.

"Wow," Jen said. "It ate it all at once!"

"I've seen it before," Jondu said in a low voice. "That owl will digest everything except for the bones and fur, then puke them back up later." She'd found owl pellets and dissected them. Found tiny teeth, vertebrae still connected in a line, even bits of straw and sticks. Fact of mountain life. Everything had to eat.

"Yuck."

Jondu held a finger to her lips.

"What? That's a Pensworthy, right? They don't eat one-spirits."

The owl pivoted its massive head. Jondu gasped and clamped a hand over Jen's mouth. The large avian head swung the other way. While they watched, the owl continued to hunt, repeating the swoop, drop, kill, and swallow. Five times. How much could one owl hold?

A faint call sounded in the distance, filtering through the trees. The owl swiveled its head, then lifted off again. This time, it didn't hunt.

Jondu watched the owl until all she could see was a fine wiggling line.

"That was dumb." Jen picked her way from the briars. Thorns tore at her jacket and pack.

Jondu joined her.

"We could've signaled that owl." Jen plucked briars from her sleeves. "Gotten a ride to the base, instead of all of this exhausting duck-walking."

"Couldn't risk getting caught up in the feeding frenzy," Jondu said. She secured one of the pine-branch snowshoes that had slipped askew. "With these thick jackets and packs, we might look more like a couple of fat rodents than skinny one-spirits." She took a moment to check their position against the boulder archway.

"C'mon. Let's move. We're burning daylight."

Chapter Twelve

Several hours passed before Taproot stood at the edge of the landfill with Elsbeth perched on one shoulder. Other than a hawk sweeping the area from high above, nothing moved.

Elsbeth untied her scarf and used it to cover her head. A brisk breeze whisked ice-glitter from the evergreens. The dump didn't ooze its usual noxious odor. Instead, the chilled scent of pine boughs filled the air. She removed one glove long enough to use two fingers between pursed lips for the one-spirit call. *Fee—fee—feeeee!*

No answer.

"If any one-spirits were here, they'd answer." Fresh alarm clawed its way up her chest and lodged around her heart.

"Time to signal for help," Taproot said. "Might want to protect your hearing, Princess."

Elsbeth wiggled her chapped hand back into the glove and covered her ears.

The mountain man cupped his hands around his mouth. *Wooo—hooo! Woooo-hooo-hooo-hooo!*

The owl call rang out across the landfill and faint hoots echoed back. Silence again.

Wooo-hoo! Wooo-hoo-hooo-hooooo! Taproot repeated.

"Bet that scared the beejeebies from the dump rats." Elsbeth lowered her hands. She loathed rats, with their nasty coats and hard black eyes. And those teeth! Too many times, back in New Haven City, she had cowered in back alleys infested with rat packs. Now that she was much smaller, she liked them even less. Elsbeth favored anything that would send them deep into the garbage and away from her.

"Upsetting the rats is not my goal. If there's a Pensworthy prowling its territory, I might arouse its curiosity. They protect their hunting grounds."

Elsbeth pondered. "I don't get it."

Taproot walked over to a boulder, scraped aside the crust of snow, and sat down. "We need another set of eyes, ones that can watch from above." He took a handful of chopped hickory nuts from one pocket, offered some to Elsbeth, then popped the rest into his mouth. Frost painted the hairs around his upper lip. "Four one-spirits don't *just* disappear."

Elsbeth stuffed down the edgy feeling prickling the skin on her neck. A huge bird sailed from the evergreens, barely moving its wings. Elsbeth instinctively dove back into Taproot's pack.

"You can come out, Princess."

She peeked over the edge of the pack. A majestic owl—clearly a Pensworthy—perched on a low branch and settled its wings.

Taproot bowed. "Genevieve. Thank you for answering my call."

The owl blinked, pivoted her head, and scanned the boulder field before replying, "My pleasure. Though I'm surprised to see you," the owl focused yellow eyes on Elsbeth, "and the little one-spirit, out before the spring thaw."

Taproot pulled at his beard. "If not for our current dilemma, I'd be snug and warm until this ghastly last breath of winter blew past." He supplied the story in a few sentences. Pensworthy owls seldom had patience for drawn-out tales.

"Haven't seen any of your one-spirits. A few fox, deer, rabbits." The owl hesitated. "There was a lowlander through here a couple of days back. Spotted his camp smoke."

From Taproot's expression, Elsbeth gathered the old man didn't like the sound of a rambling lowlander *and* four missing clan members.

"Could you pass the word amongst your peers?" Taproot asked. "I'd be in your debt."

Genevieve opened her beak and then closed it. "Tapswillowipahzkroot, there is no debt between friends."

Elsbeth seldom heard anyone attempt to pronounce Taproot's real name, proof the mountain man and Pensworthy owls' bond extended many years.

The owl tipped her head once, then lifted off. Gone, in seconds.

"What shall we do now?" Elsbeth asked. The last weak beams of sun filtered through the trees.

"What would you have us do, Princess?" Taproot asked.

Oh, no. Time to *dig within* again. Last time Elsbeth did that, her decision hadn't turned out well. "I don't . . ."

"When I'm gone on my walkabout, you *must* think for yourself."

"Why can't you use your magic, find out where they are, and zap them back to the clangrounds?" Elsbeth asked.

"Doesn't work that way. But . . ." He picked up one rounded rock and studied its slick surface. "I might be able to sense them."

Taproot held his hand over the rock's ice-slick surface. "Sim," he intoned. The ice shimmered. Strips of wire came into hazy focus for a beat, then went black. "Grant," he said. The surface remained black. The mountain man took a deep breath. "Jen." An image appeared—a view through trees thick with snowdrifts. "Ah, now we're getting somewhere. "Jondu. Show me Jondu!" The image shifted, but looked much the same. Acres of evergreen and barren hardwoods and snow.

"What does it mean?" Elsbeth asked. And why hadn't the old magician used this talent earlier? As soon as the question appeared, Elsbeth knew the answer. Because Taproot used magic as an aid, not a prop. Best to lean on one's natural senses. Magic could mislead. But it sure would be easier.

"Sim and Grant . . ." He hesitated. "Jen and Jondu seem to be traveling." He swept his hand across the frozen landscape.

"Let's go find them!" Elsbeth jiggled.

"Think, Princess."

It would be dark soon. Even now, travel would be hard in the woods. Elsbeth touched her jacket over the spot where Jen's birth crystal rested. Should have left it with someone, back at the clangrounds. No, it was up to her to protect Jen's spirit-daughter. "We'll have to build a fire. Make camp for the night."

"And then?" Taproot prompted.

When they left the landfill, which direction should they take? "Back to the clangrounds."

Taproot nodded. "Good call."

Elsbeth's eyes burned with tears. "But Sim and Grant, and Jen and Jondu are still—"

"Out there, somewhere. Yes."

Elsbeth snuffled. Wiped her runny nose on her jacket sleeve.

"Sometimes when you've done all you can do, you must have patience." Taproot stared out across the hills. "The Pensworthy owls are on the alert now. We've enlisted help from intelligent creatures more advanced, better able to cover more ground."

Taproot moved to a place guarded by boulders on three sides. He kicked at the remains of a lowlander's campfire, harrumphed. "Let's gather any wood we can. Might as well build our fire in this same spot."

Elsbeth scrambled to the ground and picked up twigs. Taproot gathered larger fallen branches. He used two pieces of flint to spark the twigs, then gradually added larger pieces until a warm fire crackled.

"Did I ever tell you about the time my circus dwarf pack got thrown in jail?" Taproot settled back, his socked feet toasting by the embers.

About a million times, Elsbeth thought. "Maybe, but tell me again."

She closed her eyes. Taproot's low voice looped around the fire, calming her uneasy thoughts. Elsbeth dreamed of riding the night wind on silent wings, rising far above the mountains, watching for her missing family with keen yellow eyes.

Sim woke. Where was he?

He blinked and waited for his eyes to adjust to the low light. One of the benefits of spending a great deal of time underground: he could see with little illumination. Thin metal bars surrounded him. A stack of cloth formed the bed where he lay. Sim scanned the cage—not much larger than his own burrow. A small can held water. Another, a mounded pile of something. He licked his lips and rose, slipping toward the side of the cage where the containers rested. So hungry, but thirsty above all. Sim leaned down to drink, then stopped to search the room beyond the cage.

Clearly, he was still in the army building. Same scent of lowlanders. Tall ceilings. Instead of the rows of cots in the last room, this one held lines of shelves stacked with boxes and cans. Like the clan's store rooms. Only, it didn't smell of dried herbs.

The room was quiet. Sim inched toward the front of the cage, to a locked swing-style door.

Have to stay alert, he coached himself. The first chance, he would escape. His stomach growled. His mouth felt so dry. Maybe a quick sip of the water. If the soldier had wanted him dead, he would *be* dead, right? Thirst drove Sim to the container. He drank and drank. Might as well eat too. He dove one hand into the mound of some kind of nuts and crammed them into his mouth. *If I'm poisoned, at least I'll die full.*

Weariness draped over him like a warm cloak. He reclined on the bedding. Just a few minutes of rest wouldn't hurt. In seconds, Sim fell asleep again.

Sometime later, a bright light flickered to life. Sim sat up, squinting into the glare.

A soldier stepped into the storeroom. The lowlander leaned down until his face was inches from Sim's cage. "Hey, little dude." The man's voice was deep and kind. Not what Sim expected from a military type. Back in New Haven City, they barked out their words, and their tones carried heavy menace.

"Since I was a kid, I've heard stories about little people living up here in these mountains. Never thought they were real." The man's lips curled up at the edges. "But, here you are."

Sim inched toward the cage door, crouched. If the man released the lock, Sim would be ready to spring out. Wait. This lowlander had the same spiked, yellow hair as the one who took Grant. Better make nice, but how would he go about that?

When Sim didn't speak, the soldier said, "Sorry about the rations, little dude. All I had were some peanuts. The stories never said what little people eat."

At least the lowlander spoke in a language Sim understood. Sim opened his mouth. "Um." His throat clamped shut. He coughed to clear the bubble of panic. "Thanks."

"Hot dig!" The soldier slapped his hands on his thighs. "You can talk!"

Sim forced his lips to lift at the corners. "Sure." His gaze left the soldier long enough to glance over the room. A second cage! A small form lay on a bed like the one in Sim's cage, a body swaddled in bandages. Grant!

"Your friend, huh?" the soldier asked.

Sim nodded.

Grant stirred, moaned. Grew still again. Thank the Light, he wasn't dead!

"I'm Sergeant Steven Johnson. Folks call me Stitch."

"Sim." He thumped his chest with a thumb, then pointed to the other cage. "That's Grant."

The soldier pulled a metal stool into position in front of the shelf and sat down. "Well, Sim. Your little buddy Grant's going to be okay, in time."

"Are you a healer?"

Stitch tilted his head, grinned. "Guess you could call me that. Do my best, given what I have to work with here, which is generally a whole lot of nothing." He motioned toward Grant's cage. "He lost a lot of blood. Tough little dude, though." He leaned in toward Sim. "Kind of surprised he made it. His injuries were severe." The soldier's eyes were deep brown. Not as dark as Grant's, more like the woody shell of an acorn, and familiar in some way.

So many years had passed since Sim had seen his father's eyes. Before the area war turned him into the resistance leader, they had been as gentle as this lowlander's. But they soon lost their kindness. The army made him change.

Remembering his father's eyes before the war and seeing the same kindness in this soldier's, Sim trusted him a little. And that surprised Sim. "Severe injuries . . .?"

The smile faded. "Little dude lost his right leg, below the knee. Couldn't save it. Tried." Stitch wiggled his fingers. "I can sew most anything back on. That's why they call me Stitch. Done more than my share of it during the area wars. Grant's leg was a mangled hot mess. Tiny. Like trying to darn a spider web or a moth's wing." The soldier glanced toward the other cage. "I did the best I could for your friend."

Reality and sadness threatened to shut down Sim's mind. One thought slipped through the muck. "Did you . . . Did you find a pendant?"

"You mean this?" Stitch fished a nubby chain from beneath his uniform. Sim recognized the pieces of metal—dog tags, the stamped IDs worn by all soldiers. His father had worn them too. Suspended next to the dog tags, hung a small acorn-shaped crystal. Grant's spirit-son. A soft glow emanated from the pendant. Sim released the breath he had been holding.

"Found it wrapped around your friend's neck. Took it off when I cleaned him up before I took care of that leg." The soldier studied the crystal. "Had this same strange light, only much dimmer. It glowed when I held it in my hand. Stopped when I didn't." Stitch looked up. "Thought it must mean something. The little dude was bad off. Figured he needed all he had just to keep living. Decided to hang it next to me, out of sight. Whatever this thing is, it seems to need to be warm and close to something living."

Good deductions for a lowlander who knew nothing of magic. "May I have it?" Sim asked. "It's important to us."

Stitch reached for the door clasp, then stopped. He untied the crystal, looped the twine around the tip of one finger, and passed it through the cage wire.

Sim cupped the pod in his hand. A tiny fracture marred the surface. He wasn't a healer. What did he know of such things?

He knotted the twine and nestled the pendant beneath his clothing. Its gentle warmth reassured him. At least he could keep Grant's spirit-son alive. He hoped. "I won't leave if you let me out of here."

"Can't have you wandering the place," Stitch said. "You're safer in here. Some of these guys might not take to having you around."

"Not the ones in those cots," Sim said. "They're barely alive. What's wrong with them?"

"Tick fever." Stitch blew out a breath. "No cure for it. Most won't make it. Those that do won't ever be right. Goes straight to the brain. Causes hallucinations. I have to keep them sedated. When they come out of it, they go batty. One of 'em set eyes on you and you'd be squashed like a cockroach."

Sim imagined himself splattered across the slick floor. Blood and guts. He shuddered.

"And the others . . . the leaders?" Stitch let out a sharp huff. "They would capture you and send you off to some lab in the city. They'd slice you up, try to figure out what makes you tick and—"

"And my people would never be safe again."

"You have a lot of smarts for a little dude." Stitch stared at Sim for a moment, then unlocked the cage door and swung it open. "C'mon. We'll check on Grant." He held one crooked arm level with the cage.

Without hesitation, Sim jumped aboard and grabbed a double handful of the fine blond hair covering Stitch's muscled skin.

"Yowsa. Hey, those are attached, little dude." Stitch's grin was lopsided. "Ease up a tad, will ya?"

Chapter Thirteen

On the return to the home valley, Elsbeth did not speak. Every thought made her eyes water. Taproot didn't talk either. Nothing sounded except the steady *scritch, scritch, scritch* of the snow beneath his snowshoes. The birth crystal nestled beneath her robe. She cupped one hand over it and silently intoned pleas to the Light within the earth and all creatures. *Blessed is the Light. The life and the Light are one. We are the Light. We are one.* Please, please let us find them!

What had Jen said, her last words? Elsbeth repeated the phrase like a mantra. *Keep faith. Keep faith. Keep faith!*

By the time they reached Taproot's hollow, the light had faded to a dim gray. He removed his pack and snowshoes and crawled through the hidden cave entrance. Elsbeth wormed from the pack's top flap once she felt the warmth of the cave.

"Why don't you get some rest?" the mountain man said. "I need some myself."

"That's it? We just sit around and wait?"

Taproot shuffled to the hearth and stacked wood for a fire. "We eat. We recharge. And yes, we wait. Patience makes perfect."

Elsbeth wanted to screech at the old man. Instead, she spun around and left his cave, heading toward the tunnel to the clan quarters.

Her burrow usually wrapped Elsbeth in its warmth, but the hearth had gone cold. She went to work. In a few minutes, the fire crackled and a pot of chamomile tea steeped on the rock stove.

The herbal tea and fire did not soothe her. Elsbeth's body tingled, as if hundreds of tiny ants crawled over her skin.

Keep busy. That will do the trick. Elsbeth threw herself into a frenzy of cleaning. Line up the honey storage jars just so, then organize the notebooks, use a piece of flint to sharpen the pencil nubs. What now? Elsbeth searched for something, anything, to keep her monkey mind occupied. She took her artwork down, shuffled the arrangement, and rehung them on the cave's walls. She used one of the sedge brooms Mari had gifted at the last Fall Festival to sweep the packed dirt floor. She plumped the down sofa pillows, then plopped down and closed her eyes.

A small living space held benefits. Easy to warm. Easy to keep tidy, except for someone like Sim.

Sim.

Elsbeth's monkey mind scrambled again, wild and unruly. She sat up.

"I can't stay here." Elsbeth slipped on a pair of boots and left to face the others.

She walked fast, then broke into a jog past the necessary rooms and the unusually quiet rooms of her spirit-daughters. She didn't allow her eyes to glance at Jondu's and Jen's doorways. When Elsbeth reached the Common Hall, she skidded to a halt at the threshold. Five sets of eyes looked her way.

Mari pushed aside a jumble of cloth, jumped up, and crossed the room. "Oh, Elsbeth! What a relief!" She smashed Elsbeth into her arms. The others joined in a group hug that comforted Elsbeth more than a hundred hearth fires.

"I know you all want to know what's going on," Elsbeth started.

"We've plenty of time for that." Mari herded her to a cushioned sitting stone.

"But . . ." Elsbeth took the steaming cup Taka-Herb offered. "I need to . . ."

Slate sat down next to her. "We know it's dire."

Of course. Slate's visions. "Can you tell where they are?" she asked him.

Slate shook his head. "Nothing clear. Some sort of cage. Dark flashes." He held up one finger. "I *do* feel all four spirits. One fades in and out. But it *is* still on this side of the Light."

Elsbeth's insides stopped quivering. Sim, Grant, Jen, Jondu—they were alive! Though, the *fading in and out* part concerned her.

As if she had read Elsbeth's last thought, Taka-Herb said, "As soon as we have them back, I can heal that *one*."

A fresh ball of worry bubbled up, spilling over. Elsbeth covered her face and sobbed. The one-spirits gathered around her, cooing and patting, until her cries calmed to hiccupping sniffles.

"It's my fault!" Elsbeth said. "This is *all* on me."

Brick leaned down. His green eyes fixed on hers. "In any fable I pen, many factors mix into the drama. Events happen; other events follow. No one thing, no one person, is the root of all. In every story, there may be hundreds of outcomes." The scribe paused. "Life is *so* random."

"True in music too," Gabby added. He picked up one of his stringed instruments and played a chord. "Listen." He moved one finger and strummed again. The tone went from light to sorrowful. One more move, another flick of his fingers, and the sound came out cheerful.

"So we just hope for a *good* outcome?" Elsbeth dabbed her tears.

Mari's expression clouded. "Actually, we are all to blame for recent events."

Everyone turned her way.

"I don't see how—" Taka-Herb started.

Mari held up a hand. "Think about it for a moment. What makes Sim happier than anything?"

"Rocks?" Brick offered.

"Whittling," Gabby said.

"Dump-diving," Elsbeth said, rising to her feet.

"Right on all counts." Mari paced in front of the hearth, talking as she stepped. "Haven't you noticed how pleased it makes Sim when he finds material and thread for me?" She motioned to the others in turn. "Or pencils for you." Brick nodded. "Or storage jars for you?" Taka-Herb pursed her lips. "And anything you could possibly fashion into a musical instrument?" Gabby shrugged. "Mystical baubles for you?" Slate nodded. "And chocolate you, Elsbeth." Mari threw up her hands. "Admit it. Weren't we *all* thinking about what Sim would bring us when we found out he and Grant had left for the landfill?"

Mari paused for a moment, then continued to stride back and forth. "He thinks of Grant, too, and Jondu, and Jen. Especially Jen, since she loves that dump more than he does." She faced Elsbeth. "Yes, you went along with Jen and Jondu's plan to search for Grant and Sim. We all did, but this started because Sim knows how much we desire *things.* For the past few years, he has left earlier in the spring and stayed later in the fall . . . all to please our wants. It's a wonder something horrible hasn't happened before."

The clan remained silent.

"Do we really need all of this stuff?" Mari held her arms wide. "Beyond basic food and shelter and some clothing, don't we have enough?"

"We've become greedy." Elsbeth backed up and sat down on a cushioned stone. "Just like the lowlanders."

"Wow." Gabby settled down beside her.

Elsbeth remembered how New Haven City's residents sucked the life from everything they touched. Bigger, better, more!

The others found seats near the hearth. No one spoke for a few moments. The fire crackled and snapped.

"I'll make some tea," Mari said in a soft voice.

Ah, yes, the cure for every ill. Elsbeth's lips lifted in spite of her sadness.

"What do we do now?" Slate asked.

"We do the one thing we're better at than greed," Mari said. "Keep faith."

"He's waking up!" Sim hunkered down next to Grant's bedding.

Grant's eyes flicked open, then shut. He moaned and pawed at the bandages binding his injured leg.

"He's in pain. Do something!" Sim pleaded. If only he had his supplies, he could use some of Taka-Herb's numbing twitchweed salve. Then again, how would he possibly find one section of Grant's damaged leg *not* covered by bandages?

Stitch left the storage room, returning shortly with a small glass vile. "It's a big risk. I had to guess how much anesthesia to use when I did the surgery. Wasn't sure how his small body would react. Could've easily killed him."

"What is that?" Sim pointed to the vial.

"It's the heavy-duty med I use for post-operative pain. I have no clue how much, or how little, it will take."

Grant thrashed on the bedding, clawing at the stump. Fresh red seeped through the bandages.

"Can't let him go on like this. The strain could hurt him even more." Stitch pulled the clear liquid into an eyedropper. He handed a snippet of gauze to Sim. "Do your best to pry this between his teeth."

The next time Grant moaned, Sim poked the gauze into one side. A line of ropy spit hung from the corner of Grant's quivering lips. Stitch managed one drop of the liquid into Grant's mouth. Grant coughed and sputtered. The gauze slipped out. He writhed for a minute. Then his eyes rolled back in his head until the whites showed.

"What—?" Sim grabbed Grant's hand.

"Wait." Stitch recapped the vial. "He's calming."

Grant's eyes closed. His chest rose and fell.

"Guess one drop is all it takes." Stitch said. "He'll need it every four hours. This is the smallest dropper I have. You'll have to brace it against your body to squeeze the bulb. I have to tend to my patients, at least until the others return."

The others. Sim felt a sense of urgency. Had to get away from here before the base filled with soldiers again. But how, when Grant couldn't walk?

"You do know how to tell time, right?" Stitch asked.

"Sure . . . I mean, I used to know." It had been over fifty years since Sim had seen a timepiece.

When Stitch smiled, his lips went all lopsided and a dimple formed on one cheek. "Suppose they don't make a watch in your size."

Sim held out his palms and shrugged.

"I have an extra. Let me go make rounds, and I'll come back and give you a refresher course."

Rhett DeVane   *Dig Within*

Stitch left. The door shut behind him with a soft snick. Too bad all lowlanders, all soldiers, weren't like him. Sim might learn to like them.

Chapter Fourteen

Jondu and Jen had camped overnight, traveling as soon as the first sun rays streaked the eastern skies. Jondu spotted the dead ash tree, her second landmark, and headed toward it. Even with the help of the pine bough shoes, walking proved tough and exhausting. Every time she stopped, her muscles twitched and complained.

"How much farther?" Jen asked.

"One more hill." Jondu had said the same thing three hills past. Could be three more hills, or six, before they reached the army base valley. A few minutes later when she stepped next to the woodpecker-pocked ash, Jondu noted a slight clearing, then a wider trail. Should they go that way? The trail headed in the proper direction. Why not? She turned onto the new passageway.

"This is a lot easier," Jen commented.

"Yep."

In a few switchbacks, they stood at the entrance to a high pass edged on either side by steep inclines. Jondu's weary spirit crashed. All Fool's Way. She had heard stern warnings about this deathtrap from Taproot. Spring rains brought mud and rock slides. In winter, ice cracked and fell in razor-sharp sheets. Even in summer and fall, the route proved treacherous and unpredictable, as if it waited. Now thick snow blanketed the jagged rocks.

Looked peaceful. Enough to deceive anyone brazen enough to attempt passage.

"Why are we stopping?" Jen asked.

Turn around or take a chance? Jondu glanced back over her shoulder. Retracing steps meant hours wasted, time they could use to find Sim and Grant.

"When we walk through there," Jondu said in a low voice. "Be quiet. No loud voices. Nothing sudden. Get it?"

"Why—?"

Jondu stopped Jen's question with a stern expression. The *quiet rule* was a fallacy, according to the lowlander's magazine articles Brick read to the clan, but Jondu didn't want to take any chances. The glazed slopes loomed over them, waiting like the jaws of a hungry wolf. If they could slip past without gaining notice . . . Jondu pressed her eyelids shut for a moment and sent out a silent plea to the Light.

"We should stop for a few minutes. Rest. Drink. Have a bite to eat." Jondu unclipped her pack. "Then we'll press on." *That will give me time to get up my nerve*, she thought.

Lulled by tea, honey cakes, and the company of her clan, Elsbeth finally returned to her burrow well after dawn and fell into the soft down bedding. Welcome sleep.

Princess, a voice called not long after she closed her eyes. *Princess!*

Elsbeth turned over and pulled the cover over her head.

PRINCESS!

She sat up and blinked to clear her vision. That voice was not a dream whisper. She pulled on her boots and over-robe and snatched up her pack on the way out.

Elsbeth scurried through the narrow passageway connecting the clangrounds and Taproot's haven and found the old man stuffing provisions into his backpack.

"Genevieve is topside. She has word of the others." He paused. "Figured you'd want to come along."

"Yes. Of course."

Taproot led the way up the angled, packed-dirt tunnel. When they popped from the hollow stump protecting the entranceway, the owl waited on a nearby limb.

"What have you learned?" Taproot asked.

"I found Kenneth Pensworthy at a watch tree near the base. He said Sim disappeared into one of the buildings. Kenneth hasn't seen him for two days." Genevieve blinked, rotated her head to survey the area before continuing. "Sim was searching for the other small one and he didn't come back out."

"No word of Jen or Jondu?" Elsbeth asked.

The owl ruffled her wings. "No."

"At least we know where to start." Taproot pulled on his pack and signaled for Elsbeth to climb aboard.

"Won't be able to take the main path," the great owl said. "Ice slide has covered one of the high sections just north of the first hill."

Taproot tugged his beard. "Only other way is to take the side path parallel to All Fool's Way. Won't go near that treacherous stretch, for sure. But it should bring us in above the ice slide. Then we'll cut back and rejoin the main trail."

"All good." The great owl leaned forward. "I'll fly ahead, check for any hindrances. I'll keep a keen eye for the other one-spirits." Genevieve lifted off.

"Too bad we can't hitch a ride," Taproot said. "Ah, well. At least the weather's improved."

Taproot took the main game trail toward the base, then veered onto a narrow path Elsbeth had never noticed. He stopped long enough to lace on his snowshoes. "Best you slip down into the pack. This way has a number of low branches. I'll do my best not to jostle you or the pack."

Elsbeth did as Taproot asked, but peeked out through a tiny tear in the material. A good while passed before Taproot's pace slowed. He stopped and flipped open the flap above Elsbeth's head.

"Send that square black pouch my way, will you?" Taproot said. Elsbeth dove to the bottom of the pack and shoved up on the pouch until she felt it lift away from her. She climbed out and stood on Taproot's shoulder.

"One of the best things Sim ever found for me," Taproot commented. He slipped a leather strap around his neck and held the pair of field glasses to his eyes, scanning the clearing before them.

Two steep slopes coated with snow and ice rose on either side, blocking the sun. Other than Genevieve passing through the clear blue sky above, nothing moved. The wind held captive by the cliffs sang a low mournful song. Elsbeth shivered. This place gave her a sinking feeling.

Taproot's head jerked. He spun a tiny focus wheel next to one eyepiece and zeroed in on something. "There!"

He pulled the field glasses away from his face and lowered them to Elsbeth's level. "Take a gander through here. Isn't that Jondu and Jen across the way?"

Elsbeth positioned her head and looked though one lens. Tiny toothpick evergreens now appeared five times their sizes. "Wow."

"See them?" Taproot asked.

A flick of bright red caught Elsbeth's attention. She knew Jen's goofy "lucky" hat, even from a mile away. "It *is* them." A gush of excitement sent her heart into triple time.

The red-hatted figure turned their way, waved, and broke into a jerky run. Her mouth was open, and she was yelling something. The second figure paused, then followed.

Something sounded, a sharp crack like the shot from a soldier's pistol. Taproot lifted the field glasses to his eyes and rotated his head upward. *Pow! Pow!*

"Oh, no!" Taproot dropped the glasses. They bounced against his chest with a thump.

Before Elsbeth could speak, the white layers coating the slope broke away, like an eggshell dashed against a rock. A billowing ice cloud rose up at the base of the slide, lifting high into the air. Taproot slammed one hand over Elsbeth. She jostled next to his coat as he took several thudding steps into the trees.

The mountains roared with the force of the plummeting snow and ice. Elsbeth sensed the earth's quake noodling through Taproot's body.

Then, eerie silence.

Elsbeth wiggled from Taproot's grasp and stared at the scene. A large clot of snow blocked All Fool's Way. Ice dust glittered in the sun. Neither she nor the mountain man spoke for a beat. Genevieve whooshed past, low to the ground. She flew back and forth, tilting her head, then diving talon-first into the snow. Over and over again, she stabbed the surface, coming up to repeat the process.

"What's she doing?" Elsbeth grabbed the field glass cord and grunted with the effort.

Taproot snapped from shock and picked up the glasses. "Hunting. She's hunting." He dropped the glasses against his chest and swung his head left, then right. He stepped over to a small evergreen, unsheathed his knife, and sawed off a long, skinny branch. Elsbeth hung onto his collar.

"What are—?" Elsbeth asked.

"No time to waste explaining." The mountain man moved as quickly as his snowshoes would allow in the white chunks churned by the avalanche. Elsbeth saw Genevieve pierce the crust again. The owl hopped, jabbing and jabbing. Then she lifted off with something dangling from her talons.

"She's got someone!" Elsbeth beat Taproot's shoulder. "Hurry!"

Taproot picked up his pace. The owl flew toward them, swooped lower, and deposited a crumpled form in the snow. She turned back, flapped to the same area, and resumed her hunt.

The pile of material and ice moved. Moaned. Taproot scooped it up. Jondu opened her eyes. Closed them.

"The skin around her eyes is blue," Elsbeth stated.

Taproot brushed away as much of the ice as possible, then removed one of his layered scarves and cocooned it around Jondu. He slipped the bundle into his coat, near his heart.

The birth crystal next to Elsbeth's skin vibrated. Profound shock settled over her. *Where is Jen?*

Taproot shuffled forward, until he reached the area where Genevieve continued her pouncing search. He probed the snow with the evergreen stick, paced, carefully inserted the stick again. For the next few minutes, he worked a grid back and forth.

The sun dipped lower. Genevieve landed in front of Taproot. The mountain man and the Pensworthy owl stared at each other.

"What are you doing?" Elsbeth called out. "Jen is down there somewhere!" When neither responded, Elsbeth grappled down Taproot's jacket and pants and landed on the snow.

She tore into the drift, digging, digging, until her fingers turned pink. Her labored breath formed its own ice cloud.

Taproot crouched down and gently picked up Elsbeth. "Time to stop, Princess."

Elsbeth struggled against his grip. "NO!"

The wind whooshed through the pass, moaning low. Elsbeth's cries added to the sorrowful serenade.

"I hear nothing." Genevieve rotated her head toward the tree line. "There are two voles up there, cowering beneath a rock." She faced Taproot and Elsbeth. "I sense nothing else. I am sorry, little one-spirit."

So they would leave Jen here? Alone, beneath the snow? "We have to find her . . . body." Saying the word made it real. Elsbeth sobbed. The birth crystal holding Jen's spirit-daughter shifted next to her skin. She reached for it, cupping her chilled hand around its gentle heat for a moment.

"We must return to the clangrounds," Taproot said. "We have to get Jondu somewhere dry and warm."

"But . . . but . . . Jen." Elsbeth's voice stuttered. "And Sim and Grant."

"We will come back after the thaw and see if we can reclaim what we've lost. Jen has passed into the Light where all must return." Taproot squinted into the distance. Moisture glistened in his eyes. "Princess, if we don't go to the home valley now, we'll lose Jondu."

He tucked Elsbeth into his muffler and bowed toward the great owl. "Thank you, my friend."

Chapter Fifteen

Sim watched Grant breathe, slower than normal. What would Taka-Herb do? Mix some foul concoction of herbs and grasses and either rub it all over what was left of Grant's mangled leg or brew it into a tea and force Grant to swallow it.

But the healer wasn't in this room, and Sim's basic emergency kit was in his pack, shoved beneath a river boulder.

Sim checked the position of the watch's hands. The longer one had gone two complete revolutions around the center. Meant he had two more until he could place a drop of the pain liquid in Grant's mouth, not an easy feat since the eyedropper was as tall as him. Sim flicked his knife open, closed, open, closed. Wished he had a piece of wood to whittle to ease his jittery nerves.

Taka-Herb did some kind of energy woo-woo thing whenever one of them had a scrape or sore muscle. Now he wished he had paid closer attention. Sim thought back to the time he had twisted his ankle jumping down from the bee hollow tree. Taka-Herb had rested one hand on his head and one on the swollen foot. Her hands felt hot on his skin.

What the heck. Can't hurt to try. Sim shifted until he knelt next to Grant. He rested his left hand on Grant's feverish forehead. The other, he gently placed over the thick, stained bandage swaddling Grant's leg.

What now? He conjured thoughts of warm things. Rocks radiating the summer sun. Herbal tea steaming in a pottery mug. The glowing orange embers of a hearth fire.

The thoughts made Sim cozy, but his palms remained cool. Taka-Herb spoke of how energy trilled through everything like lightning. How all living things shared the magnificent current. Taproot rambled on and on about that same light, too. Maybe that was the key.

Sim imagined blue streaks hitting the top of his head, streaming down his arms, and into his hands. Were his palms a bit warmer? He magnified the intent, pulling sparks from every direction, funneling it into his body.

Blessed is the Light. The life and the Light are one. We are the Light. We are one.

Sim closed his eyes and repeated the clan's prayer until the heat coursed from his hands, and he hoped, into Grant. The birth pendant grew warm next to his chest. He peeked at the watch. Like the lowlander medicine, Sim administered the energy pulse at regular intervals. Four bursts per one revolution of the long watch hand.

A couple of hours later, the door opened a crack. Stitch stepped into the storage room. "How's our patient?"

"I think he's doing okay." Sim glanced up, then back at Grant. "But he isn't taking a lot of breaths."

Stitch unloosed a strange, tubed contraption from around his neck, stuck two prongs into his ears, and held a small silver disc in one hand.

"Wh—what's that thing?"

"Stethoscope. I use it to listen to the heart. It's a bit big for your type, but I'll have to make do."

Sim moved aside. Stitch held the disc end of the scope on Grant's body. On a lowlander, it might cover a small area, but on Grant, it reached from below his neck to the top of his legs.

"Man, the little dude's heart is beating crazy wild!" Stitch lifted the disc. "Mind if I take a listen to yours?" Sim nodded, and the soldier held the stethoscope disc over him. "Oh, okay. Yours is beating fast too. Must be a normal rhythm."

"May I listen?"

"Sure." Stitch slipped the earpieces from his head and held them over Sim's much smaller ears. "Can you hear anything?"

Sim grinned. Sounded like a family of Emerald Mountain deer dancing on a boulder. Thump, thump-thump. Thumpity-thump!

Stitch looped the scope around his neck. "Let's take a look at the incisions." He paused. "You don't have to watch if you're not up to it."

"I can handle it." If he could stroll through rotten garbage rippling with maggots, Sim could see Grant's wound.

The medic gently lifted the stump and unwound the ribbon of gauze. Finally, skin showed. "Wow. Would you look at that!" Stitch's blond eyebrows lifted.

Sim leaned over. Grant's brown skin stretched over a nub where his knee used to be. Smooth like the skin of an acorn.

"I've never seen an amputation site heal so fast."

Had that buzzing energy done all of that? Sim studied his palms. Nothing peculiar about them.

Stitch glanced up. His eyes narrowed. "What *are* you two, anyway?"

"One-spirits." Sim did his best to explain. How he and Elsbeth had once been lowlanders, like Stitch. How they escaped to the Emerald Mountains during an area war and then become little people. He left out parts, about Taproot and magic and birth crystals. Sounded too much like one of Brick's fantasy tales. Besides, just how much should he trust this lowlander?

"That's about the strangest thing I've ever heard." Stitch discarded the soiled gauze and tucked the sheet around Grant. "And I've heard some incredibly strange things."

Sim lifted his shoulders, let them fall. If he wasn't a one-spirit, Sim wouldn't believe the story either.

"Based on what I see, we can back off that pain medication." Stitch stood and stretched with a yawn. "Let him wake up on his own. I'll check back on you in a bit. A couple of my guys have gone bad." His face creased with concern. "This tick fever is killing us, left and right. And I have nothing to fight it." The medic left the storage room.

What happens when Grant wakes up? Sim worried. The boy would know part of him was missing.

Cold! So cold! Jondu thrashed against walls of something frozen. Her head pounded against the hard surface. Let me out! Let me out!

"Put a cushion beneath her head," a voice said.

Was someone else trapped too? Jondu stopped, forced her heart to calm. Had to think.

"Hands in place," the voice said.

Jondu sensed points of warmth on her body. The one at her head pulsed. A wave of dizziness passed over her like a pond rippled by a skipped stone.

"Intone with me." That voice, familiar. "Blessed is the Light. The life and the Light are one. We are the Light. We are one." Other voices joined in, some high and some low. Like music. Jondu relaxed and allowed the heat to flow through her, until the tips of her toes and fingers tingled.

Maybe this was a dream before she shifted over into that Light, where all must return. Taproot told them how death wasn't so bad, not when you stopped fighting it. How the Light came all around, and love poured inside to help you cross the barrier between *here* and *there*.

That Light would shine on her face. Fear would leave. At least she wasn't cold anymore.

Jondu opened her eyes. The clan circled her, their palms resting on her body. The Common Hall hearth flickered amber light.

Taka-Herb nodded toward the others and they lifted their hands. "Welcome back, spirit-sister."

Jondu jerked her head left to right. "Jen! Where's Jen!" She noted the sad looks that passed between the clan members. "What? What's going on?" Jondu rose up on her elbows. "Where is *Jen*?"

Elsbeth knelt. She placed a shaking hand on Jondu's shoulder. "You need to rest. We can talk about everything that . . ." Her voice faltered. ". . . happened."

Jondu sat up. "No. Now!" The buzzy feeling in her head threatened. "Please."

Taka-Herb grabbed a down cushion and lowered herself to sit cross-legged beside Elsbeth. "Jen has passed into the Light."

Where all must return.
Jondu lay back and closed her eyes.

Chapter Sixteen

"My right leg is incomplete," a voice said.

Sim jerked awake and wiped the line of drool from his face. Grant sat upright, his hands resting on the stump.

"Um . . . yeah." Sim slid across the cage and knelt next to Grant.

"*Why* is my right leg incomplete?" Grant tilted his head, his dark eyes intent. "And *where* are we?"

Sim spilled the story. For a one-spirit not experienced in providing details, he was turning into a masterful weaver of tales.

Grant pursed his lips, motioned to the stump. "This will hinder travel."

Just like his spirit-son to be stoic. Had Sim awakened to half a leg, he would've screamed louder than a ticked-off hawk. "Um. Probably will make it a little difficult."

"Then I must fashion a replacement." Grant paused, considering. Sim could almost see the gears clicking inside his spirit-son's head.

"A replacement. From what, exactly?" Sim asked.

Grant looked around the storage room, taking in every detail. "Those, there." He pointed toward the next shelf, to a glass jar filled with what appeared to be long flat sticks. "Could you fetch a couple?"

Sim shrugged. "Sure. Don't know what . . ." He stopped when Grant gave him that *look*. Sim left the cage and managed to jostle the metal lid from the container. After a few failed attempts, he wrestled two sticks from inside and dragged them back to the cage.

"Hmm . . ." Grant turned the thin flat blades, studying them from all sides. "I'll need twine."

"That, I have." Sim reached inside his jacket pocket. "Here."

Grant's gaze flicked around the cage. "My pack and jacket seem to be missing. Do you also have your knife?"

Sim handed it over. Curiosity needled him. "What . . . ?"

"You appear fatigued." Grant scrunched the bedding until he formed a prop for his back. "You should get some rest."

No use to argue with Grant. Sim's spirit-son was as unmovable as a slab of granite, the stone that had inspired Grant's birth name fifty years ago. Weariness ached in Sim's every cell. Even breathing took effort.

Sim curled up on his rolled-up jacket and fell asleep.

Elsbeth followed Jondu's movements with her eyes until she felt woozy. Jondu paced in front of the mountain man's wide hearth. Back and forth. Back and forth.

"I'm relieved you are feeling much improved," Taproot said.

"Oh, *I'm* improved. Sure." Jondu stopped long enough to slam down one foot. "But Jen is dead. And it's my fault. She won't have the chance to *improve*." Jondu spit out the word.

"Please, little one. Calm yourself." Taproot patted the cushion next to his.

"I can't just sit!" Jondu raked her fingers through her oily hair. When was the last time she washed it? Her robe appeared rumpled and dirty around the edges. "Two more days have gone by. Two!"

"Yes. I can count," Taproot said.

"And not only Jen. What about Sim and Grant?" Jondu continued. "I managed to mess that up too. Never made it to the base. Don't know if they're even there." She whipped her arms. "They could be anywhere, frozen like Jen. I didn't do anything to help them, either."

"Your drama performance is wearing me out, Jondu." Taproot raised his voice. He didn't do that often, even at his crankiest. Elsbeth stiffened.

Jondu hopped onto a sitting rock and jammed her balled fists onto her hips. Lines around her eyes attested to lack of sleep. Her lips drew into a hard, thin line.

"Guilt and worry are two of the most worthless past times." Taproot took a sip of tea. "While you're sorting blame, throw some my way. If I hadn't taught Sim and Elsbeth the joys of dump-diving all those years ago, this whole mess would never have happened."

"That's absurd," Elsbeth said.

"Is it?" The mountain man huffed. "Seems with our penchant for magic, we still savor some of the bad habits of the lowlanders. Pointing fingers and fretting never got them anywhere. And it won't help Sim and Grant." He paused. "I am greatly saddened by the loss of Jen. She was a feisty one. So full of crazy plans. I will miss her, until she greets me in the Light."

Jondu took a deep breath and blew it out. "We can't sit down here, all warm and fed, while the others are still topside."

"We can't resume the search until the passes are clear," Taproot stated.

Elsbeth picked at her cuticles. A worry habit. She clasped her hands together. "There's absolutely nothing we can do."

Taproot held up one finger. "Ah, but there is. Gather the others and bring them here."

Sim held two trimmed sticks on either side of Grant's stump and lashed them down with twine.

"Help me, please." Grant motioned.

On the third try, they managed to stand side by side. Sim tightened the twine in two places.

"Not ideal, but it will work with some tweaking," Grant said.

"Try walking." Sim still held on.

Grant rocked, testing his weight on the false leg. "Let me go."

When Sim released his grip, Grant caught his balance against the cage with one hand. By swinging the stump, he managed a few steps before turning loose. He wobbled, nearly fell. Sim reached out.

"No. I must do this alone. I have to find my center." After two laps around the small cage, Grant flopped down. "My endurance needs improvement." He studied the whittled false leg. "It would be better if it bent like my other knee."

"Maybe Stitch will have some ideas."

The door flung open.

"Good, there he—" Sim's words froze. A tall black-haired soldier leaned against the threshold, his red-rimmed eyes wild and watery.

"Yah!" The man yelled out. "Stinking rats!" He lunged for the cage.

A large fist pounded the shelf. Grant attempted to stand again, but fell back into the bedding. Sim grappled in his jacket for the knife. Gone! He spotted it beneath the pile of wood shards. The soldier picked up a broom, slamming it into the cage. Sim dove to one far corner and Grant dragged himself to the other. The broom bristles scratched Sim's face and the skin stung where the stiff straw pierced.

The broom jabbed, jabbed, jabbed. Sim heard Grant cry out.

The soldier's head snapped back and he cursed. He stumbled backwards. His body crumpled. Stitch grabbed him beneath his arms and lowered his body. The broom clattered to the floor.

Sim scrambled to his feet and ran to the edge of the shelf. The black-haired soldier lay on the storage room floor, a foamy line of spittle lacing the side of his slack face. "What—"

"Let me move this man back to his cot." Stitch pulled a syringe from the soldier's neck. He lifted beneath the man's shoulders and dragged his limp body from the room. Sim turned back, pulling at the wad of bedding.

"I'm okay." Grant shoved his way clear. "But my new leg didn't fare so well." The splint lay in shatters, its twine moorings hanging in strips.

Stitch returned. "This isn't going to work. You two can't stay on this base."

With Grant's false leg in splinters, no food, and mounds of ice and snow in their way, how could they possibly leave? Sim tasted fear on his tongue, a tang like licking metal.

The medic leaned down until his head was level with the cage. "Just got word the others will be back tomorrow. It's too dangerous for you to be here. I can't keep you hidden." He tipped his head toward the door. "I'm up to my armpits in a whole room of crazies, and I'm not making any headway against this tick fever."

Taka-Herb might be able to help if only . . . Sim stopped. What was he thinking?

"I don't know where you came from," Stitch said. "But I have to take you back there."

It wouldn't be impossible, not for a lowlander. Sim looked across the cage. Grant gave a slight nod.

Sim swallowed. Trusting a soldier. Totally. The hardest thing he had ever done.

He shut his eyes. A vision appeared. Taproot and the clan, sitting in a circle. All of them—Elsbeth, Mari, Taka-Herb, Jondu, Slate, Brick, and Gabby—holding hands in a chain and chanting. But where was Jen? The vision shimmied. A wispy form hovered behind the group. Ah, there she was. He noted the large hearth. Could almost smell the blend of herbs and honeyed cakes.

Home.

Sim opened his eyes. Looked once more toward Grant. His smile told Sim that Grant had seen them too.

"We can show you the way," Sim said. "It's not far."

Chapter Seventeen

Jondu stepped from the secret tunnel, topside for the first time since the failed rescue mission. She wouldn't allow her thoughts to drift to Jen, or to Sim and Grant. So much loss. The Common Hall was the one place she felt solace, but only for a brief respite before the memory of the missing clan members echoed in her heart.

In the past few days, the weather had shifted from brutal cold to early spring, as if a giant hand shoved the arctic winds aside and allowed warmth to flood the void. Buds tipped the branches, promising a show of lime green. Birds sent love calls echoing through the woods. In other years, Jondu had popped into this world, ready to explore, no matter the direction. To turn over logs jammed with tiny insects, sniff the first blooms, trill her fingers in the frosty stream.

Jondu hunkered behind a boulder, drawn to the rich scent of dew-damp earth. A twig snapped. A twin-pointed shadow passed overhead and rippled across the first sprigs of grass. The owl landed nearby on a low pine branch and settled its wings. She recognized the predator. Genevieve Pensworthy.

Jondu slipped from her hiding spot. "You scared me."

The owl cackled. Had she lips, she would've been smiling. "Now, Miss Jondu. You? Scared?"

It was true. Jondu The Traveler was frightened. Of the slight breeze teasing the high limbs. Of the tiny *chink-chink* of the remaining ice raining down from the trees. Of her own small shadow.

Jondu had experienced a sense of unease before, many times: a rapid heartbeat, sharpened senses, the prickle of the fine hairs on her neck. All good, for a small being who could become something's easy breakfast.

What draped her body since losing Jen was beyond normal fear. This emotion glued her feet to the dirt and closed off her throat. For the first time since she had emerged from her birth crystal, Jondu wished to hide underground and seldom venture topside.

"Are you all right?" Genevieve asked. The downy feathers around the owl's neck lifted, flicked by the breeze.

Jondu's shoulders drooped. "No. I'm not."

"The trail to the base has cleared," Genevieve said. "It's muddy and several streams crisscross the low spots. But it's passable."

Jondu didn't move. "I see."

"Will you report this to Taproot?"

Did Genevieve see through to Jondu's crumpled soul? The owl showed no sign of empathy. Why would she? Pensworthy owls feared little. Their only enemy was another owl, or a lowlander.

"I'll . . . I'll . . . sure." Jondu pivoted and dove into the tunnel, relieved to be away from the sunlight and the questioning golden eyes.

She called out before entering the magician's quarters.

"Might as well come in!" a deep voice answered. "Everyone else has barged in today, why not?"

She hesitated. Taproot sounded aggravated, the way Jondu felt whenever someone interrupted her mapping hobby. She inched forward and peered around the threshold. Taproot sprawled on his sofa, a mug cradled in his hands. Elsbeth, Taka-Herb, Mari, Brick, Gabby, and Slate occupied the sitting stones around him.

"Didn't know we were having a meeting." Jondu slid into a vacant seat.

"We weren't. We all just ended up here." The lines on The First Mother's face grew deeper. "We're trying to come up with a plan."

"Where have you been?" Taproot asked. "The others searched high and low." He waggled his finger. "It's no time to just up and disappear."

"Yeah," Gabby said, rushing to great her. "We thought you were . . . gone . . . too."

Jondu held up her palms. "Sorry. I was topside."

"What?!" a blend of voices said.

"I was taking a look around." *And getting myself more frightened about it*, she thought but didn't add. "Good thing too, 'cause I saw Genevieve Pensworthy. She said the passes are clear."

The clan, what was left of it, jabbered at once. Taproot tried to speak, but the cacophony of voices covered his words. He jerked to his feet and clapped. Everyone stopped talking and stared.

"Better. Now. Here's the deal. I'll travel to the base to search for Sim and Grant."

The rabble started anew. Taproot clapped his hands again. "Lock the lips." Silence. "Repeat. *I* will go to the base."

Elsbeth cleared her throat. Heads pivoted her way. "I'm coming too." When Taproot opened his mouth to reply, she said, "I. Am. Coming. With. You."

Taproot lifted one eyebrow. A slight smile toyed with his lips. "Is that right, Princess?"

Elsbeth stretched to her full height and pulled back her shoulders. "I *am* The First Mother."

"So you are."

Jondu scrambled to her feet and paced in front of the hearth. She halted, faced Taproot and Elsbeth. "I'm going."

Taproot turned toward Elsbeth. "I don't think . . ." The mountain man pulled his beard. "Actually, what do *you* think, Princess?"

Elsbeth sighed. All of this *digging within* was tiresome. She'd much rather Taproot decide. When he continued to stare at her, Elsbeth shifted her attention to Jondu.

Did her spirit-daughter harbor the same grinding sorrow that plagued Elsbeth's every thought? Raking through tidbits of conversations, images of those horrible moments after the massive ice cloud settled. Wondering *what if* until she wanted to jab a sharpened stick into her ears to stop the inner voice. Huddling over her art pad, scratching sketch after sketch of Jen, Grant, and Sim so she wouldn't forget their smiles. Grant's lips only tilted up a little at one edge, and he managed to look deep and thoughtful. Sim pursed his lips and rolled his eyes upward. Probably just called her Lizard the Lousy seconds before. And Jen . . .? Elsbeth drew multiple images of her first spirit-daughter, trying to capture the bouncy, boundless energy behind her impish expression.

Fresh sadness threatened to slam Elsbeth.

Action had to be the best balm.

"Jondu goes with us." Elsbeth turned to Taproot. "She *must.*"

Sim looked at Grant's right lower leg. Formed out of rubbery material, it resembled the natural left leg and foot. A sleeve at the top fastened the device to the stump.

"It's not the best prosthesis in the world," Stitch said. "But better than those tongue blades you two had tied together." He smiled. "Have to give you credit for being inventive, though."

"You must do this a lot," Grant said. He stood and balanced, then gave a thumbs-up.

"More than I'd like to count." The medic's expression softened. "Feels good to be able to do something positive." He motioned toward the door. "I haven't been able to help my guys out there, lately."

Grant took a tentative step and caught his balance against Sim's shoulder.

"Here. I forgot to give you this." Stitch handed Grant a tiny walking cane. "Best to use it for a while, until you get the hang of how your body balances on that new leg. Put it on the stump side rather than the good leg." Stitch grabbed a broom handle and used it to demonstrate the proper way to position a cane. "It'll come naturally to you after a while. Pity I can't spend more time doing rehab, but I need to help you two little dudes get home."

A weight slammed against the door. Then it opened. Stitch flung a towel cover over the cage. Sim and Grant leaned together, listening to the muffled conversation. The door snicked closed. The cover lifted.

"That was close," Stitch said.

"We'll leave tonight," Sim stated.

"No. Now. One truck just dumped off a fresh squadron. More on the way."

"Wait." Sim's gaze flicked toward the door. "Won't there be a lot of soldiers moving around?"

"I'm counting on it. Best time to walk out of here unchallenged."

"Distraction is our friend," Grant said. He pulled on his jacket. Sim did the same.

Stitch opened a camouflage-printed daypack. "Come aboard, little dudes."

They crawled inside and Sim located a couple of grommets to use as peepholes. Stitch left the storeroom and passed three rows of sick patients. Sim heard moans and cries. Some of the men thrashed on their cots. Others were unnaturally still, like that first soldier Sim had watched, close to crossing into the Light.

Sim watched the little pieces of the base he could see through the grommets. Soldiers walked by. Stitch acknowledged a few without breaking his pace. Trucks grunted noxious exhaust into the air. Equipment clanged. Everywhere, Sim saw frenzied activity and heard barked orders. The number of lowlanders swirling around Stitch made Sim's chest hurt. He spotted the edge of the forest. Almost there!

"Hey! Stitch!" a sharp voice called out somewhere behind them. "Where're you going, man?"

Stitch halted. "For a walk."

"Let me clear it with Sarge, and I'll go with."

Grant's eyes widened. Sim held a finger to his lips.

"No offense, dude," Stitch said. "But I need a break from you grunts while I have coverage in the infirmary. You guys have been out joyriding in the hills. I've been snowed in, cleaning up puke and blood." He paused. "I need some solitary. Even a couple of hours. Before I go nuts."

Grant's breathing sounded like mountain thunder in Sim's ear. Hope the soldier couldn't hear it.

"That's cool," the deep voice said.

Sim heard the sound of footsteps leading away.

"Me and the boys gonna play a few hands of poker tonight." The same voice called out, from farther away. "Catch you later?"

"You got it."

Sim held his breath. Below, Stitch's boots crunched in the ice. Sim peeked from the grommet. Where were they heading? Seemed wrong. He let out his breath.

"Maybe he didn't understand our directions," Grant whispered.

Sim considered, then answered, "Stitch is sharp. Got to be a reason why we're going this way."

Traveling in this fashion wasn't so different from when he hitched a ride with Taproot. The lowlander's strides covered ground faster, with less bouncing. Sim could get used to such ease. Stitch stopped, turned ninety degrees to the left. Sim crawled up and slipped from the pack for a better look. Grant joined him.

Stitch stood in a flat, cleared area shellacked with ice and snow. Narrow crossed stakes rose in even lines.

"Where are we?" Sim spoke in a low voice, though no one seemed to be around.

"Base cemetery."

"Oh." Sim hadn't been in too many graveyards. Once, when he was a small boy back in New Haven City, his father took him to one with rows and rows of white markers as far as he could see. Men lost in battle.

Next to the clan's home valley, a small lowlander cemetery still stood. Some of the first people to pass through the Emerald Mountains, Taproot said. But no one-spirits were buried there, or anywhere else.

"In the past year, we've nearly filled up this patch of dirt," Stitch said. "Had so many die recently, we had to stack the wrapped bodies in an outbuilding until we can bury them. Earth is frozen hard. We can't dig their graves until it thaws." Stitch walked the grounds, his head down. He stopped in front of one marker. "Timothy Barrows. My best friend. Since we were four years old."

"War is stupid." Sim clenched his teeth.

"Yea, little dude. I agree. We've managed to stall the invaders for over thirty years. And yes, it seems senseless. It is. But when something or someone threatens to wipe out your home and the people you love, you defend against it." Stitch paused. "This last army would've plowed over these hills and trashed everything in its path." He tipped his head toward the markers. "But Tim and most of *these* didn't fall because of bullets."

"What happened?" Grant asked.

"Tick fever. Tim died this past fall. Couldn't do a thing to save him. At least he didn't end up piled like cord wood. Got a decent burial before . . ." Stitch's eyes watered. From the cold, or from something else? "All those high and mighty scientists, and they can't find a cure. No matter for Tim. Too late for you, buddy." Stitch kicked a clump of ice with the tip of his boot.

Sim studied the soldier's profile. The clan had never lost one of its own. Had to be awful. He couldn't wrap his mind around that.

No one spoke for a few seconds until Stitch said, "See the small marker next to Tim's grave?"

"Yes," they both said.

"That's where I buried your little leg." Stitch motioned to a tiny cross of painted wood. "In case you ever want to visit."

Grant's brows furrowed. "Thank you."

Lowlander traditions are weird, Sim thought. Why would you wish to visit something no longer alive?

"Let's get moving." Stitch tipped his head. "You'd best get back inside the pack. Don't think we'll run up on anyone, but better to be safe."

Sim and Grant crawled into the pack and took up position next to the grommet peepholes. Soon, Sim spotted familiar landmarks. For the first time in days, he felt happy.

Home wasn't far away.

Chapter Eighteen

"We'll wait until nightfall," Jondu said. "I know I can slip—"

"Stop the yammering," Taproot said in a low voice. "I don't mind you and the Princess perching on my shoulders. I know it gets stuffy inside that pack, but your constant chatter sounds like twin hornets buzzing in my ears. Besides, voices carry in this cold air."

A shushing noise sounded. Taproot halted and they all tuned their ears to the trail ahead. Heavy steps. A two-legged creature. A big one. The old mountain man jerked his head side to side, then lunged through the snow and hunkered down behind a thick stand of laurel bushes. This time, he didn't have to warn Elsbeth and Jondu into silence.

The steps grew louder. A soldier's head became visible, and then the rest of his body inched above the line of sight. Two figures sat atop his shoulders.

Before Jondu could consider her rash reaction, she called out. Taproot held up a stop hand. Elsbeth gasped.

Jondu rappelled down Taproot's jacket and pants leg, and skittered through the depressions left by Taproot's boots. She skidded onto the trail. The soldier halted, staring down with wide eyes.

"What—?" The soldier's words stopped, cut short by the squeals from the two one-spirits atop his broad shoulders.

Sim slid down Stitch's uniform, grabbing handholds on the camo-printed material. He landed on the ground with a thud and body-slammed Jondu. "Am I ever glad to see *you*."

Elsbeth joined the two in a jiving hug fest. When they pushed apart, Jondu looked up to where Grant sat. Why wasn't he coming down? And why were they traveling with a soldier? Then Jondu took note of the strange contraption strapped to Grant. She looked at Sim.

"We have a lot to tell you," Sim said. "But I'm super glad you're here. I figured someone would search for us. Guess the weather's been too bad." He stopped. "Kind of thought Jen would come. No offense, Lizard, but you don't care much for any sort of drama."

Sadness draped over Jondu. How could she tell Sim and Grant, Jen had been part of the first failed rescue party?

Before Jondu could unglue her tongue, Taproot shuffled onto the trail and faced the lowlander. The soldier's mouth remained in its open position. Guess a dwarf with a tangled beard added the final zing to three one-spirits hugging and gabbing on a mountain trail.

Sim tilted his head and smiled. "Suppose I should introduce you, Stitch. This is Taproot. And two other one-spirits, Elsbeth and Jondu." His gaze fell from Stitch to Taproot's level. "This is Stitch. He's a medic. He saved us."

Taproot extended his hand, frowned at it, wiped it on his jacket, stuck it out again. The soldier managed to close his mouth, and bent down to shake the proffered hand.

"Appreciate your aid, Stitch. Weird name for a lowlander army grunt." The mountain man flicked a slight grin. "Reckon you're no ordinary lowlander though."

Two owls swooped down and landed overhead in a tree.

"Hey, Kenneth." Sim waved the owls to descend to lower branches. "We made it out, see?"

"Indeed." The great owl eyed Stitch, his expression guarded.

Genevieve ruffled her feathers and squawked. Sim and Jondu jabbered to the second owl.

"Wait." Stitch motioned to the tree. "You can talk to birds?"

Sim grinned. "Not just *any* birds. These are Pensworthy owls. They've been friends of ours for years."

"And of mine," Taproot added, "for much longer than the one-spirits have known them."

"Hmm," Stitch said. "I've been up here for a good while, and I've never seen one of them up close." His lips crooked into a lopsided grin. "Just when I figured talking to little people and a dwarf were sure signs I needed to check myself into a mental unit. Now I can add in little people that talk to owls."

They shared a laugh.

Taproot gestured toward Jondu and the others. "I can take it from here, Stitch. You probably need to head back."

Sim crooked his finger and the lowlander crouched down. "I'll come and see you, Stitch. I promise."

"Don't venture onto the base, little dude. Not safe." Stitch's brown eyes rested on the others. "You all are best left to legend." He paused a second. "Get close enough to call the signal, and I will meet you in the cemetery. No one goes there unless . . . Let's just say, it's not a place where people hang out." He gently lifted Grant from his shoulder and placed him on the trail next to Sim. Grant wobbled before he caught his balance with the cane. Jondu and Elsbeth hugged him.

Jondu's eyebrows scrunched together. From the looks of things, they all had stories to swap. Jen's final chapter was the worst.

"You know the call we practiced, in case we became separated?" Sim held cupped hands to his lips. *Twee. Twee. Twee.*

Stitch nodded. When he smiled in his crooked way, that one dimple dotted his cheek.

Sim held up a fist and bumped it against the soldier's much larger curled-up hand. "That's how you'll know it's me, big dude."

Two weeks passed. Elsbeth trailed after Taproot, lugging two crocks of honey. The last beams of sun painted the sky peach and crimson. The days had grown steadily longer, and the air warmed. Snowmelt flowed into the streams and ponds.

The balm of spring soothed Elsbeth. Sweet scents of new buds, the promise of life. After losing her first spirit-daughter, she needed spring. Chickweed, dandelion, brook greens. Her mouth watered for the taste of leafy plants picked fresh. She dreamed of ripe summer berries, sweetened by the sun.

Taproot whistled a little ditty. No doubt the old mountain man had brewed another of his noxious tonics for the Spring Festival of Light. Good for defeating the winter blahs and curing what ails a body, he claimed. The tonics made Elsbeth's head swimmy, and her eyes lost focus. But the syrupy red liquid did whisk away any sadness clinging to her spirit. They could all use that, especially this year. Thank the Light Taproot hadn't mentioned leaving on his walkabout.

Since their return to the clangrounds, Sim had kept to himself. Sullen, rarely joining the clan in the Common Hall, as if he couldn't bear the presence of the others. Taka-Herb brewed various curative teas, leaving the pots beside his plate. No one noticed Sim coming and going, but the food and drink would go missing later. At least he wasn't starving himself. Still, Elsbeth worried.

Grant coped with the loss of his lower right leg better than Sim. Every week, Grant appeared with a different whittled cane, modified to suit his purposes. He planned to dump-dive soon after the Spring Festival of Lights, a feat not easy even with two sound legs. Grant pondered his barriers and came up with solutions. Elsbeth noted how he practiced his loping stride, until the false leg swung easily alongside its natural counterpart.

The physical hardships proved easier to overcome than the spirit-deep scars. Time would smooth things out, Taproot assured. Maybe the Spring Festival of Light could work magic for everyone. Elsbeth hoped so.

Elsbeth set down the heavy honey crocks and rubbed the crimp in her shoulder. Slate and Gabby busied themselves gathering sitting stones, placing them in a circle around the large flat rock at the center. The animals filtered in—squirrels, rabbits, raccoons, and a couple of skunks. The frogs would show up later, and the Pensworthy owls. Some years, a troop of foxes attended.

If the clangrounds were closer to the landfill, the rats might be invited. Elsbeth shivered. All creatures deserved respect, yet she still found it hard to like rats.

Taka-Herb appeared, tailed by Brick and Jondu. The clan's healer directed the preparation of the salad and herb dishes, calling out orders in singsong. Mari carried two stacks of folded robes to a rock and plopped them down with a grunt. Grant followed, leaning on his cane in one hand, with a pottery crock of foxfire in the other. His spirit-son's birth crystal bumped against his robe, glowing with a soft blue light.

Elsbeth's hand went to the birth crystal suspended from her neck. Jen's spirit-daughter. Comforting, that a small part of Jen lived on, ready to join the clan. Perhaps fill a little of the void left by her spirit-mother's passing.

"Where's Sim?" Elsbeth asked.

"Dunno." Brick used a hand broom to whisk dried leaves from the tablerock. "Haven't seen him."

Elsbeth left the clearing. She meandered through her end of the clangrounds and the Common Hall, and stood at the entrance to Sim's private quarters.

"Hey, I'm coming in," she called out and walked through the tunnel. When she stepped into Sim's cave, she blinked to adjust her eyes. The hearth fire offered little light, and the foxfire bowl shed none of its usual green glow.

"Are you in here?" Her voice wove and bounced through the stacked rocks.

"What do you want." Sim's answer came out flat and haunted, with no lilt at the end to prove it was a question requiring an answer.

"The Spring Festival of Light. That's what." Elsbeth peered around the room, trying to figure out where Sim hid.

He stepped from behind a tower of river rock. His face did not show in the shadows.

"You may call me Lizard the Lousy, and I *am* sometimes," she said. "But I'm going to start calling you Sim the Surly."

Sim turned away and shuffled toward the hearth, where he slumped down onto a sitting stone. Elsbeth followed, feeling her way so she wouldn't topple one of the hoodoos lining the narrow path. She eased down on a stone across from him. "I miss you, Sim. We all do."

He huffed. "Like you miss Jen? Do I deserve to laugh, and eat, and drink tonic? Like nothing ever happened?" Sim raked his hands through his unkempt hair. "Like Grant still had a leg and Jen still bounced around like a maniac? Like *that*?"

"I'm sad too, Sim."

"It's all on me." His shoulders curled forward.

Elsbeth said the same words she had told herself repeatedly, until she believed them. "Jen's death was an accident, Sim. A wall of snow and ice. You didn't cause that. And Grant's leg was an accident too."

"All because *I* had to take off to dump-dive before the thaw."

"Nobody blames you."

Sim shifted to face her. His eyes glistened in the firelight. "*I* blame me." He thumped his chest with a fist.

Elsbeth stood, walked over to where he sat, and rested one hand on Sim's head. If only she could send enough healing energy to ease his pain.

"Remember when we escaped from New Haven City?" She lowered herself to sit beside him. "You were as scared as me, probably worse because of your father. But you took my hand and helped me come to the Emerald Mountains. You've always been the brave one, Sim. Mr. Adventure Man." She chuckled. "Without you, I would have never entered a landfill to search for treasure or had the courage to become a one-spirit."

"I'm not brave, not now."

"Sure you are. You just got knocked down. That's all. Heck, in all of those hero fables Brick tells, there's always a dark time when the hero stumbles. Then he comes out on the other side, even braver than before. And wiser."

When Sim didn't reply, Elsbeth stood and wove back between the rock hoodoos. She stopped by the threshold and looked back. "Please come to the festival, Sim. The clan needs you." She paused. "I do too."

Evening cloaked the mountains. Stars dappled the sky.

Taproot signaled for the group to calm. "*Blessed is the Light*," he sang in a strong voice. The first line of the song wound around the gathering, until they all joined in. "*The*

Light is with us. We celebrate life. The Light and the life are one. We are the Light. We are one."

The foxfire glowed green. Taproot nodded to Elsbeth. She stepped into the center of the ring and searched the circle of faces. If only Sim was here. Suppose it was up to her to tell the old story this year.

She took a sip of tonic and began, careful to speak slow and clear.

"Long ago, we belonged to a clan of people of great wealth, in the flatlands far to the south. Though everyone had plenty to eat, clothing, and houses, there were those who would kill for power. A time of many wars followed. Many were maimed and killed."

The clan had heard the story for years, yet they still leaned forward as if Elsbeth's words held a great secret.

"Two lowlander children, Simon and Elizabeth, escaped into the Emerald Mountains. We met Taproot." She paused to bow to the old dwarf. "He protected us and taught us the ways of these mountains, what to eat, where to seek shelter, how to honor the Light that glows within all creatures. Taproot used his magic to help us become what we are now, one-spirits. Sim The First Father and Elsbeth The First Mother. He taught us to remake our likenesses in the forms of birth crystals, and the first spirit-son and spirit-daughter were born."

Elsbeth's throat constricted with emotion. For the first time in fifty years, Jen wasn't listening to the clan history.

"So it has been for many years. We have defended our home against lowlanders who would destroy it. We live in peace and friendship with the creatures of these Emerald Mountains." She raised her hands and everyone chanted the final words. "We are the Light. We are one."

Elsbeth stepped toward the center flat rock. She slipped Jen's birth crystal over her head, kissed it, and placed it onto the rock next to the foxfire. Grant stood, steadied himself with a carved cane, and walked to the center of the ring. He removed the birth crystal from around his neck, held it to his heart, then placed it beside Jen's birth crystal.

Elsbeth reached out and held Grant's hand. Should have been Jen standing here, witnessing the emergence of her first spirit-daughter. "Please forgive me, Jen," Elsbeth whispered. The night wind answered with a low sigh. Words echoed in her mind: *Forgive yourself.*

Taproot joined them beside the flat rock now, holding up his hands. He intoned a series of senseless words.

What kind of language? Elsbeth wondered, as she had every ten years. She reviewed their foreign sounds in her mind. Sure, she could repeat them, but what did they mean?

The foxfire glow intensified. A mist swirled up from the rock, burst overhead, and showered down. The clan *oohed* and *ahhed.* The animals chattered. Kenneth and Genevieve Pensworthy *wooo-whooood.* The light shimmered into a dome, arching to the level of the treetops.

A snap drew Elsbeth's attention. Grant squeezed her hand. A second *pop!* In the center of both crystals, tiny cracks appeared until they broke into halves. Two tiny creatures stepped out. Grant's spirit-son looked up to his spirit-father. The child's red hair flashed like a hot flame, a brighter shade than Brick's. His skin, pale as moon glow. Grant would have an interesting task, choosing a name for the striking creature.

The second one-spirit lifted her eyes to regard Elsbeth. Elsbeth's mouth dropped open. The little one resembled Jen, with the fair skin, pale hair, and bright blue eyes. A sense of peace and hope surrounded the child, as if she already understood the secret to overcoming pain and suffering.

Jen's last words echoed in Elsbeth's memory, the ones she had said when she handed over the birth crystal to Elsbeth's safekeeping. *Keep faith.*

Elsbeth smiled. Naming this one would be easy.

"Welcome to the world, Faith."

Chapter Nineteen

Elsbeth trilled her fingers across her new robe—buttery linen printed with pale flowers, trimmed in bits of lace. Mari had fitted all of the clan members with new summer attire, her Spring Festival gift. The others shared personal gifts, as they always did at the spring and fall parties. Taka-Herb with her teas, Jondu with unusual seed pods or bits of twisted wood, and Grant with glossy pictures he gleaned from dump-dive magazines. Everyone jiggled when Slate shared his summer predictions: a new bee hollow two valleys over, the promise of a patch of dewberries not far from the old dump. Brick read his latest great tale, mimicking recent events. He left out the sudden death of one brave explorer. Fiction could do that: smooth over the hard parts.

As she stacked the empty pottery bowls, Elsbeth hummed the melody of Gabby's tune, a winding ballad that had made them laugh, cry, then laugh again. Music, how could they move forward without it? The tone and words expressed the sadness they shared with the first death of a one-spirit. She glanced to the basket holding Sim's robe and gifts and wondered if he would rejoin festivities by the fall. Sure, they all felt loss, but gathering with the promise of spring and the new births helped ease the pain.

The empty sitting stone Jen usually occupied still graced the ring. Small flowers, rocks, and tributes lay at its base. Elsbeth closed her eyes and sensed Jen's spirit. Peaceful, for once not agitated and wild.

"The celebration was a success." Mari gathered the two youngers to her. "I'm glad Taproot suggested we leave Jen's place in the circle. Seemed right."

Elsbeth opened her eyes and nodded. For the first time since the avalanche, tears didn't stain her cheeks. Her lips lifted into a smile when she looked down at Faith and Zeke.

Unusual name, Zeke. Elsbeth expected Grant to follow Sim's lead and name the younger after some rock, or wait until the younger's personality dictated a title, as it had with Gabby. Instead, Grant chose a biblical name, Ezekiel, shortening it to Zeke. Grant related the story of the Old Testament prophet, how Zeke's scarlet hair reminded Grant of Ezekiel seeing a "ring of fire." Would Zeke be a prophet like his namesake? Two seers in one clan would take some getting used to.

Outfitted in much smaller robes than those of the older one-spirits, Faith and Zeke would live with Mari for a couple of seasons until the rabbits carved new quarters. Mari wished it so, and everyone voted approval. Though Faith could occupy her spirit-mother's burrow, the clan had agreed: Jen's quarters would remain vacant, a sanctuary for all to share.

By the fall, the youngers would achieve full height. Unlike lowlander offspring, Faith and Zeke possessed the collective knowledge of the clan, yet no spoken language. They would greatly benefit from Mari's guidance before they took independent roles in the clan.

Elsbeth smiled, remembering the past, how she had once worried about Jen's and Grant's lack of speech, how the youngers talked when they were ready, and in full sentences. Jen, especially, took to the spoken word and rarely remained silent. Fifty years of memories waited for Elsbeth to revisit Jen's life. But for now, spring and summer beckoned.

Mari left with the two youngers. Other than Taproot and Jondu packing empty tonic jars into a basket, the clearing grew quiet. One of the Pensworthy owls called nearby, probably shopping for a fresh kill to supplement its festival meal.

"I'll be on my way, first thing in the morning," Taproot stated.

Elsbeth dropped a stack of bowls onto the tablerock with a clatter.

"And I'm going with him." Jondu faced Elsbeth, her arms akimbo.

"No! Absolutely not!" Heat rose in Elsbeth's cheeks.

"I'm a traveler." Jondu thumped her chest with one thumb. "Have been since I stepped from the Light." She leaned forward, fixing The First Mother with a stare. "Should I not become more of what I *am*?"

"But . . ." Elsbeth took a shaky breath. "You *will* . . . return?"

Jondu let out a belly laugh. "That's what travelers do, go and come back. Can't move too well in the winter." Her expression clouded briefly. "I can come home in the fall."

Useless to argue. "In time for the Fall Festival?"

"Sounds like a plan." Jondu hugged her spirit-mother.

Taproot grunted. "Suppose you might have consulted me before you made this announcement." He hung the loaded basket on his arm. "At some point, our paths will diverge. Me to seek Dell-Fee, and you toward . . . where?"

"The deep mountain clans of Dena and Zackary," Jondu answered. "I've studied the old maps, and I'm positive I can find them."

Elsbeth forced a deep inhalation. Blew it out. Moments like this, she forgot to breathe.

"You've no experience with long travel. You'd be safer here," Taproot said.

"And how do I gain such experience, huh? Not by tramping the same worn path back and forth to the landfill." Jondu lowered her voice. "And what is truly safe?"

Truth settled on Elsbeth's shoulders. Was this the way of parents, letting their children go? If not now, when? *The perfect time to do a thing is seldom perfect.* Brick wrote that in one of his fables.

Taproot waited, tapping one foot. Honestly, if he told her to *dig within*, Elsbeth would stomp on his toes. She took a moment to make sure of her words.

"Jondu will go, Taproot. She *has* to."

The fabric roses Mari pinned onto Jondu's pack stuck out like tree lichens. Jondu tapped one lacy bud with her finger, shrugged, then hugged Mari. "Um . . . Thanks."

According to the two rough-drawn maps that Jondu had studied far into the night, a couple of rivers and various feeder streams blocked the route to the deep mountain clans.

Elsbeth and Taka-Herb fretted with last-minute additions to Jondu's provisions. Every member of the clan had stopped by with some small bauble to stuff into the bulging pack. *Too bad I can't train one of the Pensworthy owls to fly this stuff ahead for me,* she thought.

Elsbeth stood back, wringing her hands. "Are you sure about this, Jondu?"

"Yes." She was more than sure. "Determined. Delighted. Excited."

"Okay then." Elsbeth turned toward Taproot. "And you? Will you return in time for the Fall Festival?"

The mountain man yanked his beard. "Long's the way, and long's my stay." He shouldered his pack.

Jondu looked skyward and puffed out a breath. Maybe parting company with the riddling magician wouldn't be so bad after all.

"For *how* long?" Elsbeth asked.

Taproot leaned down, until he was eye to eye with Elsbeth. "You can handle things here, Princess. Remember—"

Elsbeth held up a stop hand. "I know. I know. *Dig within.*"

"Maybe you can get Mari to stitch those words onto a robe," Taproot said with a chuckle. "Wear it around like a cloth tattoo." He ignored the stink-eye Elsbeth sent his way. "Ready, fellow traveler?" he asked Jondu.

Jondu endured one last round of smashing hugs. She tipped her head toward the north and gave a sharp nod. A Pensworthy owl performed a flyover, dipping one wing in salute. Jondu thought it might be Kenneth. Hard to tell. No matter. It was good to know she and Taproot would cross the Emerald Mountains under the watchful eyes of a friend.

Elsbeth stood, rooted in place, staring at the spot where the forest had swallowed Taproot and Jondu. With one last wave, they had vanished—the old magician who taught her and Sim the ways of the mountains, and her spirit daughter, Jondu The Traveler.

"May the Light follow and shield them," she whispered. The brush rustled behind her. Elsbeth whipped around.

Slate dashed toward her and bent double, sucking in gasps of air. "Sim! Sim . . . is . . ."

Elsbeth rested a hand on his shoulder. "Steady. Breathe. In. Out. In. Out."

Slate closed his eyes and released a slow exhalation. "The First Father is gone."

"Figured Sim wouldn't wait much longer to dump-dive." Elsbeth glanced toward the clear spring sky. A few high clouds scudded past. The trees budded in shades of lime green so bright, the colors stunned her eyes.

Slate shook his head. "No. I mean . . . he has moved from his burrow."

"Impossible!" Where would he go? "It would take a lowlander dump truck to cart all of his rocks."

Slate nodded, pursed his lips, then shook his head. "All the important stuff is missing." He frowned. "I don't know why I had no visions about this."

After one final, longing glance toward the north, Elsbeth trailed Slate through the tunnels to Sim's private quarters. The moment she entered Sim's burrow, she noticed the difference. A dead, deserted sensation. Stale air. No hearth fire. Only the foxfire offered a meager green glow.

She wound between the rock hoodoos. None of them seemed to be amiss, but could she tell if they were? The burrow looked like its usual jumbled mess. Elsbeth scanned the room. Sim's packs did not hang in their customary spot, and his favorite hiking stick was missing.

"I don't get why you're so upset." She pointed to the corner. "He normally takes the same stuff every time he goes dump-diving."

"He didn't ask any of us to go along."

No surprise there, either. Not since Jen's death. "Oh, I wouldn't worry—" Her words stalled in her throat when she noted the mantle above the hearth.

Sim's most cherished possession—a hunk of obsidian darker than a moonless night—no longer occupied the place where it had rested for nearly fifty years. Elsbeth crossed the room and ran her fingers across the vacant spot. Her spirit dropped.

"Sim *is* gone." Elsbeth shouldered past Slate, stopping outside of Sim's burrow long enough to whistle *twee! twee!*

Since Elsbeth and Slate were closest to the Common Hall, they arrived first. Slate took his usual seat at the tablerock. Taka-Herb and Mari rushed in, followed by Brick, Gabby, and Grant. Each slid into their customary positions and looked toward Elsbeth with concern. The "all-out" call had been used only three times in fifty years. The two youngers perched on Mari's shoulders, watching with wide eyes.

The clan felt depleted without Jen and Jondu. Now, even more without The First Father staring her down from his side of the table. Thank the Light for Faith and Zeke.

Sim has left us. The depression of the past few weeks joined hands with this fresh blow. Elsbeth wanted to crumble into a heap and sob.

Dig within, Princess. The words sounded in her mind, as if the old mountain man stood by her ear.

"Who has seen Sim?" she asked.

"He came to my burrow . . ." Taka-Herb tapped her temple. ". . . two days ago. Wanted to replenish his supply of healing salves."

Brick spoke up, "I saw him early yesterday morning. He took a crock of sourwood honey and some cakes." He thought a moment, then added, "He had a bag he filled with nuts and dried fruit, too. Didn't think much of it. Sim's been taking his meals to his burrow since . . ."

Elsbeth sighed. Questioning glances flicked around the group. "Anyone else?"

Mari picked at a loose string hanging from her sleeve. "He's probably gone to the landfill. You know Sim."

"I thought that too, at first." Elsbeth explained about Sim's missing belongings.

Grant stood and walked over to the hearth. "I should've seen this coming." He stared into the flickering flames.

Elsbeth joined him.

"The First Father came by my burrow before the Spring Festival. Said he accepted blame for Jen's death, for my leg. I tried to assure him, to tell him . . ." Grant's voice cracked. "I—"

Elsbeth rested a hand on Grant's shoulder. "I said the same words."

The others murmured behind them.

"Sim's told us all about his crushing guilt," Mari said. "He didn't trust what we told him, that no one blamed him. Not at all."

"Hard to believe someone else, when you no longer believe in yourself," Gabby said.

Slate held his hand over his chest. "What can we do? We have to *do* something."

Faith climbed down from Mari's shoulder and stepped to the center of the tablerock. She spun in a slow circle, looking with earnest eyes at each of her elders. The chatter stopped.

"Find Sim," the fair-haired younger said, her voice soft. "Ask him to come home."

Silence ruled for a beat. Youngers rarely spoke before six months had passed. This one had been on this side of the Light for less than twenty-four hours.

Elsbeth shook off her disbelief and refocused on the problem. "Where do we start to look?"

Brick rapped his fist on the table. "I vote for the landfill."

"Maybe the base?" Slate offered.

Grant held up one finger. "I think I might know where Sim is."

"Then I'll go find him, plead with him to come back." Elsbeth turned to Grant. "Tell me."

"Better, I show you."

"But, your leg."

Grant fixed her with a stern look. "My leg is not a hardship."

Elsbeth gave a definitive nod. "Get your pack. Meet me topside."

Chapter Twenty

Jondu and Taproot stood on the east bank of a wide waterway, the largest Jondu had ever seen. She consulted the tattered old map from Taproot's collection. "The Oriah River." She glanced up. "And I thought Mad Woman River was big."

"Rather intimidating. Rather swift." Taproot removed his pack and used it as a seat. He pulled out a packet of dried fruit, tore off a leathery section of plum, and handed the rest to Jondu. "Suppose there's a way to cross without ending up with our brains smashed against the rocks?"

"Or losing a leg like Grant did." Jondu unpacked the second map and rolled it out beside the first. She chewed on the plum, tracing her finger across the yellowed paper.

"Here." She pointed to a tiny mark across the Oriah River's broader blue line. "Bet it's some kind of bridge." Jondu tapped the map. "We're about here, so . . ." Her gaze lifted toward the north, ". . . the bridge or whatever should be upstream."

Unlike the brooks near their home valley, the Oriah River rolled between steep banks lined with boulders and towering pines. The spot where they rested contained pebble-sized stones, a good place to find a perfect treasure for Sim. Jondu made a small x on the map. She could stop on the way home. *Wow*, she scolded herself, *here I am barely two days into the journey and already thinking of the return trip.*

"Searching for a safe bridge sounds like a plan." Taproot stood, stretched, and pulled on his pack.

For the next hour, they traveled a switchback course, running as parallel to the river as possible. Jondu hustled to keep up with the dwarf's pace. At the crest of a hillock, the twisted riverbank came into view.

"I see the crossing," Taproot said. "Not much farther." He moved forward at a fast clip until he reached the cluster of boulders.

Jondu caught up with him and studied the natural bridge. Two massive rocks on opposite sides of the river leaned toward each other, positioned as if some giant hand had plopped them down.

"Space between them looks to be about five feet. I can jump that. Crawl aboard." Taproot tapped his backpack.

"No. I'll be doing this by myself on the way home. I have to figure this out." Jondu crouched down, her chin in her cupped hands. "I have an idea."

Taproot waved one arm. "Be my guest."

Jondu tied one end of her dump-dive rope around a small rock and whipped it in a circle until it gained speed. She released the rope, holding fast to the free end. The first try, the rock bounced off the other side and splashed into the river. Jondu reeled it in. It took two more casts before the weighted rope looped up and over the branch of a pine on the opposite bank.

"What now?" Taproot's eyebrow lifted.

"I swing like the ape man guy in one of Brick's dump-dive books."

"Tarzan?"

"That's the one."

"I don't . . ."

Jondu grabbed the rope. She took several steps back, then ran toward the Oriah River, swinging into the air in a low arc until she landed with a thud on the opposite side.

"Whoop! I did it!" Jondu pumped one arm in the air. "Want me to throw the rope back across for you?" She called out.

Taproot shook his head. He backed up, got a running start, and leapt easily across the chasm. He leaned down and held up his palm. Jondu slapped it.

"And what does your map tell you now?" the mountain man asked.

Jondu studied the drawing. The crosshatches marking the deep mountain clangrounds lay to the left. The red star

Taproot had added to denote Dell-Fee's camp lay across the page in a different direction. She looked up. "I think . . ."

"This is where we part ways, Jondu The Traveler." Taproot tipped his head. "May the Light watch over you, little one."

"And you." Jondu noticed the old dwarf's eyes. Were those tears?

Taproot blinked, sniffled. "Consider limiting your journey to the night hours, when you have the protection of the Pensworthy owls."

"Yes," Jondu said. "Figured I'd find a good place to make day camp and start up again at dusk."

"And don't eat unfamiliar berries unless—"

"I notice the birds and squirrels eating them. I know. I know."

The one-spirit and the mountain man regarded each other for a moment before Jondu spoke again. "I hope you find your friend Dell-Fee."

"Give my regards to the clans of Dena and Zachary." Taproot nodded, gave his beard a tug.

Jondu kicked rocks with the tip of her boot. Were they going to stand in this spot the rest of the day?

The old dwarf spun around and stepped into the deep brush. Gone.

Jondu was alone. Truly alone. For the first time in her life.

A branch snapped above her head. She dove beneath a pine seedling, then peeked up. A Pensworthy owl stared at her from a dead hickory limb.

The corners of her lips curled up. Not *totally* alone.

Elsbeth watched Grant struggle with his left leg. The trail had provided an abundance of obstacles—downed limbs, rocks, pockets of mud. Now, they faced the sheer rock wall leading to Taproot's watchtower. To her, the steep path stretched beyond the planets. No telling how it appeared to Sim's first spirit-son.

Grant led with his sound right leg, pulling his weight up until the prosthesis rested next to his natural leg. Bits of loose gravel skittered to the ground far below.

"Maybe . . ." Elsbeth closed her mouth when she noted Grant's slumped shoulders. Defeated: she had felt that emotion.

Grant stared down at his legs. "I may need more practice before I can conquer Taproot's watchtower." He tilted his head back to regard the slit in the rock face above them. "To think, Sim and I scaled this path a few weeks ago with little thought to the difficulty." He pivoted to look at Elsbeth. "My current reality fails to meet my high expectations."

Elsbeth offered a sad smile and a nod. So like Grant to take momentary failure in stride.

"I can describe the position of the blind cavern," he said. "Sorry I can't take the lead."

"We don't know if this is where Sim has moved."

Grant held up a finger. "It stands to reason. Sim often told me how he came here to seek solitude. Plus, the cavern would provide adequate shelter from the elements."

"True." Unless Sim had been secretly excavating a new burrow, a natural enclosure made perfect sense. Grant outlined the landmarks leading to the cave. Elsbeth repeated his instructions twice to make certain she understood.

"I'm not so good with directions." Elsbeth shrugged.

Grant's eyebrows lifted.

"Like that's a surprise," she added. Her lack of an inner compass provided the stuff for endless ribbing by the clan. Elsbeth knew up and down. Side to side. But north, south, east, west? Each direction looked the same. She navigated by familiar tree stumps, fern beds, and the shapes of hills.

"I'll descend and await you." Grant held out his hand. "Let me have your pack. The reduced weight will make your ascent easier."

She shucked her backpack and started the climb. Heights bothered Elsbeth more than directions. Better to be snug underground than clinging to some lofty cliff. Owl-gliding was different. Sitting securely atop a Pensworthy owl, Elsbeth experienced the joy of flight.

Focus on one step at a time, she coached herself. She reached a stunted pine clinging to a small patch of dirt between boulders and searched the rock behind it. There! She squeezed through a narrow triangular gap. A cave spread out before her, long and slender, with tumbled boulders forming the walls and ceiling.

She waited for her eyes to grow accustomed to the meager light, then looked around. Sitting stones, a rock hearth. Stacks of stone hoodoos. Like Sim's burrow.

Elsbeth noted a clump of some sort. She slipped across the cave and leaned down. When she touched the crumpled mound of cloth, it shifted. She jerked her hand away. With the tips of two fingers, she lifted a corner of the blanket and peered beneath. Sim shivered and moaned. A smudge of blood stained one corner of his lips. One hand clutched his chunk of obsidian.

Sim's eyes opened to slits. "Tick . . .tick," he said. "Tick." His eyes rolled back in his head until only the whites showed.

Tick? She didn't understand. Her mouth went dry with worry. Elsbeth tucked the soiled covers around Sim. "I'll go get help."

Elsbeth searched for another blanket. When she found none, she removed her jacket and placed it over the top of Sim's shivering body. "Hang on, Sim. Please, hang on."

She descended twice as fast as she had climbed, oblivious to the dizzying height this time. She thumped to the ground. Grant opened his mouth to speak, but Elsbeth held up a hand.

"Got to go get help. I found Sim and something's really wrong. All he says is *tick, tick*, over and over."

"Tick fever." Grant's expression grew stern.

"Is that bad?"

"Very. Kills lowlanders. No cure." Grant glanced down the path and let out a sigh. "I'll wait here. I'll only slow you down."

Elsbeth cradled Sim's chunk of obsidian in her hands. As soon as he was well—and he *would* get well—she would give it back. It could return to its proper place on his mantle.

Taka-Herb's burrow smelled of rich earth, herbs, and warm honey, a blend of scents that never failed to calm Elsbeth. She needed calm, especially now. She huddled beside the hearth with her arms wrapped around her tucked knees. The fire sent waves of warmth through her.

The medicine woman handed Elsbeth a hot cup of chamomile tea. "Sim's sleeping, finally. I know you, Gabby, and Slate did the best you could to make the trip home easy for him. Quite impressive, the idea for getting him down that rock cliff."

Elsbeth nodded. "Grant came up with the plan while I ran for help." The cloth and rope sling with Sim cushioned inside reminded her of a cocoon, and it had worked well to lower him to the ground.

Mari eased down next to Elsbeth and put one arm around her shoulders. "Please, go to your burrow and get some rest. Taka-Herb and I will stay with Sim."

The thought of leaving Sim, even for a moment, steeped Elsbeth in dread. "I can't! No. I'm fine. Really." If she was laying on that cot, freezing then burning, Sim would never desert her. As long as Sim got well, he could call her Lizard the Lousy every day until the Fall Festival.

Taka-Herb stood at the stone stove, pitching ingredients into a stewing mix of mulled herbs. "Sim said something odd. Made me think."

How anyone could understand Sim's garbled speech amazed Elsbeth. She and Mari leaned forward, intent on Taka-Herb's words.

"He said, *Deer not sick*." Taka-Herb tore off a clump of wild onion and added it to the pot. "Clear as day."

"What does it mean?" Mari asked. "Makes no sense."

"Perhaps it does." Taka-Herb crushed red berries and stirred them into the bubbling liquid. "If this illness strikes the lowlander soldiers, and they're calling it tick fever . . ." She wiped her hands on her apron. "The rest of us don't visit that part of the valley, haven't for years since the barracks went in."

"But Sim does," Mari stated.

"Right. And none of us have this disease." Taka-Herb gave the pot a stir.

"Grant was with him," Elsbeth said.

"And didn't get bitten." Taka-Herb warmed to the theory, stirring faster until the broth frothed. Elsbeth had not seen the healer this intense since two springs past when Jondu discovered a patch of wild ginseng. "If the deer, or other animals, don't fall prey to this tick, they must be eating something that offers them protection."

A flicker of hope rose inside Elsbeth.

"I'm mixing every herb, grass, and berry the deer eat. Some of these only grow next to where the old dump used to be, before the lowlanders filled it in and put up the army base. I'll distill an elixir and give it to Sim."

"And if . . ." Mari started.

"If it doesn't help, I'll keep tweaking the herbs until something does."

Chapter Twenty-one

Elsbeth woke with a jerk and swiped the sleep drool from her cheek. For a moment, she watched the fire licking the hickory logs. Other than an occasional sizzle-pop, Taka-Herb's burrow was quiet. Mari napped on the couch beside her, her lips curled in a peaceful smile. Good thing the two youngers were with Brick and Slate in the Common Hall.

Across the room, Taka-Herb ministered to Sim. For two days and nights, the medicine woman had worked, brewing elixirs and dripping them into Sim's slack mouth. Still, his fever raged.

Taproot's seer's stone bumped against Elsbeth's leg. She slipped it from her robe pocket and rolled it in her palm. *Wonder if I can work this?* Taproot said it was "all about intent." No problem there. She had a wish list overflowing with intent.

Elsbeth stared at the rounded rock's slick, black surface, allowing her eyes to shift off-focus. Nothing happened at first. Then a fuzzy form shimmered in the middle.

"Wow," she mouthed.

The dim outline faded. She tried again, this time willing her mind to tune into the image. Hold it. Hold it.

A view of rolling green hills spread out before her. Trees stretched wooden arms toward a sky dusted with feathery clouds. Elsbeth willed the seer's gaze to look down. Jondu's sandaled feet appeared, crusted with a scrim of trail dust.

It works! The sudden thought caused the vision to jiggle. Elsbeth calmed her mind and the scene cleared. *Deeper sight, please,* she asked the stone. Colors popped—verdant clumps of grass with light painting the blades, a dragonfly perching on a spike of wild peppermint, and the chocolate and gray of a Pensworthy owl, its warm weather plumage.

Emotions filtered from the stone, filling Elsbeth with wonder, joy, and a sense of well-being.

Jondu The Traveler is happy! Elsbeth squelched the urge to clap and jump up and down. She wondered if she could reach Taproot and shifted her thoughts toward the old magician.

Nothing.

Elsbeth tried again, pushing the intent hard. Her temples pounded.

The stone remained dark. What did it mean?

A shuffling noise announced Grant's arrival. He entered the burrow, cast a quick glance toward the couch to Elsbeth and the still-sleeping Mari, and crossed the room to Taka-Herb. Elsbeth eased from her position. Mari mumbled and turned over, but did not wake. Elsbeth padded to join Grant and Taka-Herb.

Grant pulled a packet from his robe. "I found these growing near the base." He poured several wine-colored berries into his palm.

"You went there? By yourself?" Elsbeth pinched her lips together.

Grant squared his shoulders. "Had to do something to help. Couldn't just sit in my burrow."

Before Elsbeth could work up a scolding reply, Taka-Herb reached for the berries. She studied them, rolling them in her cupped hand with a flick of one finger. "Where did you locate them, exactly?"

"West bank, near the point where the lowlanders used to dump their ruined automobiles."

"Never seen this variety in our part of the woods," the medicine woman stated. "Did you take note of any creatures eating them?"

"The rats." Grant thought for a second. "And a rabbit."

"So they're not poisonous. Rats will eat most anything, but they're not stupid." Taka-Herb dropped the berries into the simmering elixir and gave it a stir.

Elsbeth's heart thumped. "Wait! You're going to give those to Sim? They could . . . They might . . ."

Taka-Herb faced Elsbeth. "Kill him. Yes." She tipped her head toward the cot where Sim lay. Sim's chest barely rose and fell. His skin, gray and mottled. He already looked dead. Elsbeth blinked back tears.

"He hasn't eaten or taken fluids for over two days," Taka-Herb said, "and we don't know how much longer he went without nourishment before we got him home. None of my herbs conquer the fever for more than a few minutes."

Elsbeth and Grant stood side by side, silent.

Taka-Herb breathed in, then released the air in a long sigh. "I don't—*we* don't—have any options left."

Brick slid a plate of acorn flour pancakes in front of Elsbeth. Normally, she would tuck into the hot cakes covered with honey and walnuts. She pushed the plate aside. Her stomach felt as unsettled as her spirit.

"We all think you need to eat," Brick said. The others sitting at the tablerock nodded.

"If not," Mari added, "Taka-Herb will have one more to doctor."

The two youngers watched Elsbeth with intense eyes.

Elsbeth moved her head up and down once. Had to set a good example for the youngers, at least. She picked up the fork. The first bite nearly choked her, as if her throat had forgotten how to swallow. She took a quick swig of now-cold rose hip tea and coughed. Tried again. The blend of warm honey and pancakes worked magic. Elsbeth polished off the short stack and used the last forkful to sop the excess honey.

"You can't change anything except your attitude," Elsbeth said in a low voice.

Gabby glanced up from his plate. "Hmm?"

Elsbeth waved one hand. "I was talking to myself. Just something Taproot once said."

"I do that a lot. Sing to myself, too." He wiped his mouth, pushed back from the table, grabbed up his doo-brood, and strummed a few chords.

"Pretty," Mari said.

"I'm writing a song in honor of Sim. Wanna hear?"

Slate stifled a burp. "What, like you don't expect him to . . . make it?"

Gabby's mouth twitched. "No. I mean, *yes*, I do expect Sim to live. Music takes my mind off dark thoughts. When I create, I focus on the good."

"Got an idea." Brick grabbed a pad of paper and pencil. "Let's tell some funny stuff about Sim. I'll write about them. Or Gabby can use them to compose his ballad."

"What kind of stories?" Jondu asked.

"Like when he got into scrapes and came out okay," Brick said.

"There are so many." Mari chuckled. "Hard to know where to start."

Elsbeth touched the dump-dive heart locket. "All the times he passed out, overcome by dump gases. The time the bees stung him so many times, he nearly quit breathing." She hesitated. "When he tried to fly using a stupid contraption of tulip poplar leaves and twine."

"What about the time he shot the falls in a raft of twigs?" Brick said.

Slate laughed. "Remember when he tried to harvest porcupine quills to make some sort of spear weapon? That critter didn't take kindly to Sim."

Grant smiled, nodding. "Or when the snake shared his burrow for months, but he didn't know it because of all of those rock hoodoos?"

The stories flowed around the clan. Zeke and Faith listened, their eyes wide. Elsbeth had to admit that the remembrances chased the distress. Her stomach unclenched and the weight of dread suffocating her breathing eased.

Taka-Herb rushed into the Common Hall. Talk ceased.

"Sim's awake!" Taka-Herb held a hand to her chest and breathed. "He's asking for you, Elsbeth."

Elsbeth pushed back from the table and followed Taka-Herb to the burrow. When they entered, she saw Sim propped up on pillows, his eyes open for the first time in several days.

"Hiya, Lizard." Sim's voice cracked.

"Oh, thank the Light! You're okay!" Elsbeth rushed across the room and leaned down to give him a hug.

"Why wouldn't I be okay?" He coughed. Took a sip of water. "How come you got your scales all ruffled up?"

Elsbeth plopped down on the sitting stone next to the cot. Sim's grin brought life to his pale features.

Sim wobbled when he stood. Interesting, how a few days spent horizontal had turned his strong leg muscles into pond goo. No wonder Stitch and the lowlanders hated the tick fever illness. Besides the fact that it killed them.

"I came close to entering the Light," Sim stated.

"Yes, you did." Taka-Herb held out the cup with the cure, mixed with honeyed tea.

Sim sniffed the brew and scowled. "Do I still have to take this nasty stuff?"

"A couple of days more, to make sure. We'll all add the berries into our diets going forward." She jabbed a finger toward the mug. "Drink."

Sim held his nose and slugged down the liquid. *Gaaahhkk!* He danced a jig.

Taka-Herb laughed and took the cup from Sim. "Saved your life, this swampy drink."

"Bet you can't make it again."

"Bet I can. I carefully recorded each ingredient and how much I added. Important when making a new tonic. Afraid I'm not as good as Taproot. He threw in a pinch of this and a handful of that, and his cures turned out perfect every time." She handed Sim a second cup. "I must measure and write down my recipes."

Sim fired the stink-eye at the mug. "More?"

"It's lemongrass tea, to take the moldy taste from your mouth."

He took a sip. A fresh scent like summer sunshine eased aside the odor fouling his nose.

"Better?"

Mmmmmm. Sim took his time with this mug. When Taka-Herb turned her back to stoke the hearth fire, he shoved the tick fever cure recipe into his robe pocket.

Rhett DeVane   *Dig Within*

Chapter Twenty-two

The next day, Sim slipped from the clanground using the secret exit in the boys' necessary room tunnel. It took him three times longer than normal to reach the army base. He stopped to rest after every four switchbacks. Even downhill proved a challenge.

"I *will* get better," he muttered. "No stupid tick fever's going to slow me down."

As if the ghost of the illness still hid deep within his cells, one of Sim's leg muscles cramped. He hobbled to a rock, sat down, and massaged his calf until the muscle relaxed.

Two grueling hours later, he stood at the edge of the base cemetery. Kenneth Pensworthy flew past, dipped one wing, then landed high on a dead tree limb. Always a comfort to have a watchful sentinel, especially now when Sim's body did not respond swiftly.

The grave markers stood, dark reminders of death. The place possessed an odd hush, as if a cloak of silence draped across the disturbed dirt. At least the lowlander soldiers had markers where they rested. Unlike Jen, whose remains lay scattered atop a steep pass, at the whim of tons of ice and snow.

Sim shook off the blue thoughts and cupped his hands around his mouth. The signal cry echoed through the valley. He waited. Called again.

For the next hour, Sim emitted the summons. A figure slipped from the pines. The spiked, yellow hair showed white in the moon glow.

"Stitch!" Sim tried to run, but his legs would not cooperate. He slowed to a lopping walk. "Yo! Stitch!"

The soldier whipped around to face Sim's call, flashed the beam of a small flashlight his way, then clicked it off. They met between the rows of crosses.

Stitch crouched. "Hey, little dude." The medic held out his hand and Sim shook one of Stitch's fingers. "Good to see you, buddy."

"Likewise." Sim shucked his pack and used it for a seat. For the next few minutes, the two friends swapped stories.

"Things aren't going so well here." Stitch tipped his head toward one corner of the cemetery where freshly turned dirt mounded in dark humps. "Losing soldiers left and right to tick fever. Our ranks are so depleted, we'd roll over if we came under attack."

"That's why I'm here." Sim stood and dug in his pack. He handed over a slip of folded paper.

"What—?"

"It's a copy of the recipe for a cure our healer made for me."

"Wait, you?"

Sim nodded. "I got it. Was bad sick for days. The bite *still* itches. But I didn't die. This stuff did the trick."

Stitch unfolded the paper, flicked on his light.

"I wrote the letters really big so you could see them."

"What are these? Firebrand? Feverspike?" Stitch's eyebrows furrowed. "Never heard of them."

"Plants and stuff that grow near here." Sim handed over a vial. "This is a bit of the elixir Taka-Herb made."

Stitch held the tiny container between a finger and thumb. "If I can get this sample to a lab, maybe they can isolate the chemicals." He palmed the vial and slipped it into his uniform pocket. "Scientists have to be good for something."

"Soon as the sun comes up, I can point out the plants."

"If this works for us like it did for you, you'll be saving a lot of lives, little dude."

Rock hoodoos lined the stream near the clangrounds, reminding Elsbeth of a glossy picture in one of Brick's magazines. The lowlanders called it *land art*. Cliff sides draped with ripples of colorful canvas, or strange sculptures plopped down to blend with nature. Not meant to be permanent, instead to live in the moment, reflecting the surroundings.

"Who put these here?" She turned toward Grant. His spirit-son skittered between the rock piles. Faith hid behind one tower and lunged out at Zeke. Both youngers giggled and started the hide-and-seek game anew.

"I found them yesterday as Zeke and I gathered brook lettuce," Grant said. "I need to show you something else, too." He crooked one finger toward Zeke and Faith and they followed him toward the tunnel entrance. Elsbeth took one last perplexed look at the hoodoo garden and fell in behind Faith.

Grant stopped when he reached the threshold of Sim's burrow. "Get ready for a shock."

The first thing Elsbeth took note of was the fresh lemony scent. The air lacked the stale heaviness she associated with Sim's private quarters. Above, the bottle skylights sprayed light into the space. No dust or soot there. The second thing she noticed—the clean-swept dirt floor.

"So, that's where the rocks came from." She pivoted to take in the entire room. No clutter. No top-heavy piles of sticks. No whittled wood filings. "Has he moved out, again?" The thought of Sim in a rock cave alone crimped Elsbeth's spirit.

Grant stepped to the hearth and pointed to the single object atop the mantle. "Don't think he's gone."

Sim's favorite chunk of obsidian rested in the center of the shelf. She lifted the stone and a piece of paper fell to the floor. She picked it up and read aloud, "Will be back."

Grant took the note, turned it over twice as if it held a deeper, hidden meaning.

Elsbeth blew out a breath. "Why does everyone in this clan keep leaving? Where has he gone this time?"

Faith tugged on Elsbeth's sleeve. "I know something."

Elsbeth crouched down to face Jen's spirit-daughter.

"Taka-Herb said the recipe for her cure was missing."

Grant clapped his hands together. "I know where he—"

"The base. Sim's gone to the base." Elsbeth closed her eyes. Maybe when she opened them, Sim's burrow would be crammed with stones and sticks, and he would be standing there calling her Lizard the Lousy and wondering why she was ruffled.

She opened her eyes. *Oh, well.*

"I'll get my pack. Go after him." Grant started toward the tunnel.

"No!" Elsbeth's voice echoed. Faith and Zeke looked at her, their mouths open. Grant halted and turned around. His brows tilted up.

The truth settled around Elsbeth's heart. "It's okay. I think Sim *needs* to be a hero."

Chapter Twenty-three

Elsbeth chose a sun-warmed boulder with the best view of Mad Man's Pass. Nearby, Grant and Mari helped Taka-Herb harvest the last of the huckleberries. The days grew shorter, a bit each day. Small signs indicated the approach of fall. Leaves blushed, then turned brown and released their grip. The clan and the mountain animals moved with intent. Get ready for winter!

Zeke and Faith's blended laughter trilled like music, and she imagined the two youngers darting between the trees, popping out to scare the fur from unsuspecting squirrels. Good thing they could play. The young one-spirits would soon grow as serious as their elders.

The Emerald Mountains rippled in the distance—dark to paler in color where they greeted the horizon. No matter if she reached three hundred and fifty like Taproot, Elsbeth would never tire of this view. As they had the first time she and Sim had seen them, the ancient hills cradled her, soothing away the sadness of the past few months.

When your troubles pile up, count your joys. Taproot's words rang in her memory. She squinted into the sun. Where was the old magician? Something warm brushed her shoulder. She jumped and looked around. Nothing there but a beetle trailing across the stone.

Oh, he was still on this side of the Light. Out there, somewhere. She turned back to take in the vista.

And Jen floated above. At peace. Elsbeth sensed her essence too.

Maybe she should use the seer's stone, look deep into its shiny surface for hints about Joudu, Taproot, even the spirit of Jen.

No, she decided. Sometimes it might be better to allow her heart to feel the way.

At the clangrounds, preparations were underway for the Fall Festival. As happy an occasion as the Spring Festival, it heralded the abundance of the harvest, and gratitude for the food and shelter the earth provided. Everyone anticipated the night of feasting and laughter. The telling of the old tales. The gift-giving.

Except for Sim.

He lived in his burrow, grabbed meals, then left with no explanation. Elsbeth and the others asked no questions. Mari, always the peacemaker, urged patience. But Elsbeth's patience wore as thin as her summer robe.

A shadow blocked the sun. Elsbeth gasped and dove between two rocks. She peeked out from her hiding spot, then stepped out and stood with her arms crossed over her chest.

Kenneth Pensworthy stared at her with round yellow eyes. "You must be more watchful, First Mother. I could've been a hungry red-tailed hawk."

"But you're not." Elsbeth scrambled back into her position on the boulder. "Guess you're right. The beauty of all of this," she swept one hand toward the hills, "distracted me."

"Ah," Kenneth chattered. "Easy, on such a fine, cloudless day."

"Have you seen Jondu?"

The large owl pivoted his head, scanning the valley, then turned to face Elsbeth. "No."

Elsbeth's shoulders slumped.

"But there are a lot of hills out there, First Mother, and so *little* Jondu."

Sim heard the echo of stomping steps before he saw their owner. One thing about the hollowed-out burrow: no rock piles to snuffle sound. Elsbeth stormed through the doorway and crossed over to where he stood, next to the hearth.

"Lizard, what—"

"Do you plan on taking part in the Fall Festival, or what?"

"I don't think I—"

Elsbeth's loud huff stopped his words. "This has gone on too long, Simon."

His lowlander name hung in the air, a phantom from New Haven City with its dark, rat-infested alleys.

"That's right. You heard me. I called you *Simon*. Because you're not Sim. Not *our* Sim."

He backed up and lowered himself onto a sitting stone. Elsbeth didn't often show fire, but when she did, it was best to hunker down and let her burn herself down to an ember.

"You moved back. Sure. But not really." Elsbeth took in the burrow with the sweep of one arm. "Not that I mind actually being able to breathe in here, and I'm glad you cleaned up a bit, but . . . Really, Simon? It's like you've ripped the heart from this burrow, from this clan, from yourself!"

He waited. Was she finished?

Elsbeth sucked in a breath. Sim braced for another barrage. Then her shoulders curled forward and she sank to sit cross-legged in front of him. Tears spilled down her cheeks and she smashed her face into her cupped hands and wailed. Horrible, gut-ripping, girl sobs.

Sim could deal with Lizard the Lousy, even Lizard the Loud, but not this version. He got down on his hands and knees and inched toward her, in case the lunatic Elsbeth still lurked.

Elsbeth lifted her head. Her cheeks glistened.

"It's like—" Sim stretched to find the words. "—like it makes me feel better to be here, but . . ." He paused. The fire snapped and sizzled. "It hurts too. I did things that caused Jen to die and Grant to lose his leg. And everywhere I turn, something reminds me."

"I made mistakes too." Elsbeth offered a sad smile. "Sim." She swiped a damp hank of hair from her eyes. "I will—we will—make more mistakes. I miss Jen, too. Crazy miss her. But she's living in the Light now."

"How do you know that for sure?" Sim asked in a low voice.

Elsbeth patted her robe above her heart. "I feel it, in here."

They sat for a moment before Elsbeth said, "You took Taka-Herb's elixir recipe to the lowlanders, didn't you?"

Sim nodded.

"Did it help?"

"Stitch says it may cure tick fever, eventually. The formula isn't exactly right for lowlanders, but at least they are no longer dying."

"Thank the Light," Elsbeth said. "You want to atone somehow, make it all okay. I understand. Trust me, I do. But when will it ever be enough, Sim? When will you feel—"

"Like I deserve to be alive?"

She reached over and grasped his hand. "Come back to us, Sim. Please, come back."

Jondu plucked rounded pebbles from a small pond. Perfect for Fall Festival gifts. Sim would be thrilled. The rocks held a mottled, green cast not seen in their valley rocks. This crescent-shaped pool, the same one she had passed five months prior, was not marked on either of her maps. Either the previous travelers weren't so great at map-making or Jondu had bumbled onto a new landmark. She used a stubby pencil to sketch on the parchment.

"I'm officially naming you Lost Lake," Jondu announced aloud, to the surprise of the two squirrels burying acorns nearby. A turtle lifted its head and slipped off the log where it had been sunning. Jondu watched the ripples fan out from the spot where it had plopped into the water.

Lost Lake. A fitting name, since she had managed to stay lost most of the summer. Sure, she might have begged directions from Genevieve, to point a wing toward the Deep Mountain clans. The great owl checked in with Jondu off and on, before moving to better hunting grounds.

But no. If any traveler was going to locate those other one-spirit clans, it would be her. She would do it by herself, even if she had to start all over this spring, and the one after that.

Jondu checked the position of the sun. Two hours until it painted the sky red and orange. The traveling would grow more difficult in the deep woods, but slightly less dangerous at the same time. No need for the constant vigilance against the day predators.

She stored the pebbles in her pack and brushed dirt from her hands. According to the markings she had left when she passed this way before, many hours of hard day and night walking lay ahead if she wanted to reach her home valley in time for the Fall Festival, and she still had to cross the Oriah River.

Jondu shifted her pack and tightened the cinch line.

No time to waste.

Chapter Twenty-four

Mari set down a stack of thick winter robes and rested one hand on Elsbeth's shoulder. "She'll come. You must believe."

Elsbeth blinked, turned to face Mari. "What?"

"You've been staring at that one corner of the clearing since we came topside."

Elsbeth took note of the festival preparations. Taproot usually carried the tonics, most of the food, and directed placement of the tablerock. Not this time. And still . . . things moved smoothly. Every clan member pitched in.

Grant stepped beside them. "How many sitting stones shall I put into place?"

"Twelve smaller, and one large one," Elsbeth answered. "Then plenty for any animals that might show up." The squirrels, raccoons, and rabbits were as dependable as the afternoon showers, but who knew if the foxes and frogs would appear? The opossums might trundle by for a moment or two, but they preferred their meals rotten.

Grant scrunched his eyebrows together. "Thirteen stones?"

"No matter if Sim, Jondu, and Taproot aren't here, I want seats placed in their customary spots. Select a special one for Jen. She will always be a part of this clan, no matter that she now lives in the Light. Put Faith next to me, and Zeke by you. They act up when they sit together." Elsbeth chuckled. "Besides, Mari can probably use the break."

Grant touched his hand to his forehead in a quick salute, then moved away to oversee the seating arrangements.

Taka-Herb appeared at the periphery of the circle, heaving three crocks of amber liquid. She slid them off the shoulder harness with a huff, then ambled over to their group. "Sure hope the tonic turns out right. Tasted a little off to me. Guess I don't quite have Taproot's recipe mastered. It's drinkable, but there's a little aftertaste of—"

"Snail spit," Faith provided. She stood beside the medicine woman, grinning.

Elsbeth ruffled Faith's fine, yellow hair. "Never tasted snail spit before."

"And neither has this one." Taka-Herb put her hands on Faith's shoulders and swiveled the younger ninety degrees. "Go see if Slate and Brick need any help setting the tablerock."

Faith scurried away. "That child is too smart for her own good," Taka-Herb said. "She's already committed most of my cures to memory. Guess I have an apprentice, whether I want one or not."

In a few minutes, the sun dipped low in the sky. Elsbeth's favorite time of day, the gloaming, when faces turned to outlines against the fiery sundown and the night creatures shifted in the forest. Where were the Pensworthy owls? Should be here by now. Ah, well. That's how it went, when you threw a party in the Emerald Mountain woods.

No telling who, or what, might show up.

Elsbeth raised her arms into the air, the signal for calming. The clan—minus three and Taproot—looked her way and the animals stopped their chatter. For the first time since she and Sim had escaped into the Emerald Mountains, no Pensworthy owls watched from the pines.

The First Mother pushed disappointment aside. *Dig within*, her inner voice coached.

"We thank the Light for the harvest. For friendship, for love, for family." She closed her eyes. Her voice quivered at first, then grew stronger.

Blessed is the Light. The life and the Light are one. We are the Light. We are one.

The old song lifted her. Voices joined in. Without looking, she picked out Mari's sweet soprano, Taka-Herb's alto, and the fresh voices of Faith and Zeke. Gabby's folksy bass thrummed beneath Brick's slightly off-key alto. Slate's song sounded ethereal, as if the Light itself filtered from his throat.

Another tone joined in, one so familiar Elsbeth instantly pegged its owner. She opened her eyes.

Sim met her gaze from the edge of the foxfire's glowing ring. He stepped into the circle. Other voices faltered. Elsbeth's throat constricted and she closed her mouth. Tears washed her cheeks.

The clan grew silent, waiting. Sim spread his arms and tipped back his head. He sang the old song, alone at first.

Then a second voice echoed from the darkness.

Elsbeth tore her gaze from Sim and searched the shadows. Could it be? Her heart thrummed.

Jondu The Traveler emerged from the forest. She crossed the clearing to the Festival circle and dropped her packs. Two Pensworthy owls swooped low then lifted to perch nearby. Silent sentinels.

Sim and Jondu harmonized. One by one, the clan members joined.

Elsbeth clasped her hands together. Her joyous voice blended with the others, lifting into the Emerald Mountain night.

Blessed is the Light. The life and the Light are one. We are the Light. We are one.

THE END

Did you enjoy *Dig Within*?

Please visit the book's Amazon page and leave a quick review.

***Elsbeth and Sim*, Book One of the Tales from the Emerald Mountain series, is available in Kindle and print versions with online vendors.**

About the author

Rhett DeVane is a true Southerner, born and raised in the Florida panhandle. For the past thirty-plus years, Rhett has made her home in Tallahassee, located in Florida's Big Bend area, where she splits her workdays between her two professions: dental hygienist and author.

Rhett is the author of five published mainstream humorous adult fiction novels set in her hometown of Chattahoochee, Florida, a place with "two stoplights and a mental institution on the main drag": *The Madhatter's Guide to Chocolate*, *Up the Devil's Belly*, *Mama's Comfort Food*, *Cathead Crazy*, and *Suicide Supper Club*. She is coauthor of two novels: *Evenings on Dark Island* with Larry Rock and *Accidental Ambition* with Robert W. McKnight.

The *Tales from the Emerald Mountains* series is her first middle grade fiction.

To learn more about Rhett DeVane and her writing, visit her website: www.rhettdevane.com

www.ingramcontent.com/pod-product-compliance
Lightning Source LLC
Chambersburg PA
CBHW051833170626
46807CB00003B/1160